The Science Contest

Hilary Dennis

Published by Bright Minds Books, 2024.

While every precaution has been taken in the preparation of this book, the publisher assumes no responsibility for errors or omissions, or for damages resulting from the use of the information contained herein.

THE SCIENCE CONTEST

First edition. November 5, 2024.

ISBN: 979-8227603791

Written by Hilary Dennis.

Table of Contents

Description

The Science Contest follows the transformative journey of two high school students, Dan and Brenda, who embark on an unexpected mission to make clean water accessible.

After developing an affordable filtration system for a science fair, their project rapidly gains attention, leading them from local contests to national recognition and international partnerships. Facing relentless challenges and inspired by the communities they aim to help, Dan and Brenda turn their vision into PureWater—a sustainable organization bringing change to underserved regions.

This inspiring story reveals the power of youth, resilience, and innovation to address real-world challenges and impact lives.

Dedication

To all young dreamers and creators, who see beyond obstacles and dare to change the world—this story is for you. And to communities around the world, whose strength and resilience inspire us to innovate and serve. Finally, to every mentor, teacher, and supporter who believes in the potential of others, thank you for fueling the fire of possibility.

Preface

In *The Science Contest*, I wanted to capture the unique intersection of youth and purpose—what happens when curiosity meets a deeply rooted need, and the incredible transformations that follow.

Dan and Brenda's journey is inspired by countless young people who channel their talents toward meaningful causes, often without the certainty of success. Their story explores not only the triumphs of invention but also the essential failures and growth that accompany bold undertakings.

The Science Contest is both an adventure and a tribute to those who see solutions where others see problems. May it inspire you to find, nurture, and follow your own mission.

Chapter 1: The Spark of an Idea

Dan Carter loved efficiency. Whether it was the way he organized his notes, his precise time-blocked schedule, or his step-by-step approach to assignments, everything in his life was ordered. The last thing he expected was to find himself paired with someone as vastly different as Brenda Collins.

Brenda didn't believe in schedules or rules, at least not in the same way Dan did. Her notebooks were filled with doodles, messy scrawls, and hastily written ideas crammed between the lines of actual class notes. Creativity wasn't a trait she aimed to hide; rather, it shaped every aspect of her. So when Mr. Thornton assigned them to be partners for the upcoming science project, Dan didn't know what to expect.

"Look, Dan," Brenda said as they sat across from each other in the corner of the school library, "if we're going to work together, we need a project that's more than just another science fair cliché. I'm not interested in making a baking soda volcano."

Dan's gaze shifted from his notes to Brenda. "Good. Neither am I." He adjusted his glasses and continued, "I was thinking about something that has practical value, something useful in the real world."

Brenda's face lit up. "You mean something that could help people, right?"

"Exactly," he replied, taken aback by her sudden enthusiasm.

She thought for a moment before speaking, her voice almost a whisper. "What about water? Clean water, to be specific. We take it for granted, but I read a report about towns not too far from here struggling with polluted drinking water. Something's got to change, don't you think?"

Dan paused, thinking it over. The topic was huge, but the idea had potential. He took a deep breath and looked her in the eyes. "That's a big issue, Brenda. But maybe we could create a small-scale solution, something people could use to filter water on their own."

Brenda leaned forward. "What if we could make it affordable, too? Something people could build with easy-to-find materials? We could create a prototype here, and if it works, well... who knows?"

Dan's mind was racing. The thought of developing something with a true purpose was thrilling. "Let's start with the basics, then," he said. "If we're serious about this, we need a solid foundation. Research, materials, feasibility."

Brenda smiled, her energy uncontainable. "Dan, I think we just found our project."

With their partnership sealed, they started dividing tasks. Dan would handle the technical aspects, while Brenda would focus on the design and practicality. They knew they would need their teacher's approval, and that meant crafting a clear pitch.

The next day, they met up in Mr. Thornton's classroom after school. The room was empty, save for Mr. Thornton himself, who sat at his desk grading papers. He was the kind of teacher who encouraged questions and took genuine interest in his students' ideas, no matter how unconventional.

Brenda took the lead. "Mr. Thornton, we have a project idea. It's about creating an affordable water filtration system for areas with limited access to clean water."

Mr. Thornton put his pen down and looked at them with interest. "That sounds ambitious. Why a filtration system?"

Dan spoke up, feeling a mix of excitement and nerves. "Because clean water isn't as accessible as it should be, even here. We've read that many households still rely on outdated filtration methods, or worse, have no filtration at all."

The teacher considered their words, nodding slowly as he processed the concept. "It's a noble cause," he finally said. "But I have to ask, how would you go about making it affordable and accessible?"

Brenda was ready. "We'd use sustainable and readily available materials. Our idea is to test with things like activated charcoal, sand layers, and possibly local resources for filters. We'd like to build a prototype to show how it could work in a small setting."

Mr. Thornton's eyes sparkled with curiosity. "I like the ambition. But you'll need more than just enthusiasm. A project like this requires careful planning, testing, and patience. Think about it—is this something you're both prepared to commit to?"

Dan and Brenda exchanged a glance, each silently reassuring the other.

"Yes, sir," they answered together.

"Well, then," Mr. Thornton said, rising from his seat, "let's see a plan by next week. I want to know the materials you intend to use, your budget, and any preliminary research you can gather."

As they left the classroom, Brenda let out a sigh of relief. "That went well. I thought he'd shoot us down immediately!"

"Mr. Thornton's tough, but he's fair," Dan replied. "He's right, though. This will be a lot of work."

Brenda waved off his concerns. "We've got this. Imagine if it actually worked! People could have cleaner water, and we'd have accomplished something meaningful. This is going to be amazing."

For the next few days, they worked on gathering preliminary data and testing out the potential materials. The library became their second home as they poured over scientific journals, engineering books, and online articles about water filtration. Dan compiled data on the properties of various materials, while Brenda focused on how they could fit together in a functional design.

They quickly realized their biggest challenge: striking a balance between cost and effectiveness. Some of the best materials were too expensive, and the more affordable options didn't meet their criteria for effective filtration. Frustration set in, but they pressed on, determined to find a solution.

One afternoon, Brenda looked up from her notes. "Have you thought about activated charcoal? It's cheap, easy to find, and it absorbs impurities. It's not perfect, but it could be a start."

Dan jotted down the idea, his mind already working through the mechanics of incorporating it into their design. "We could layer it with sand and gravel, using gravity to push the water through."

Brenda grinned. "And if we use some kind of natural filter, like cotton or even fabric scraps, to catch larger particles, that could be our first layer. A simple, three-step filtration process."

Excitement buzzed between them as they visualized the design. They'd need to test it, of course, but the outline was there, ready to be built upon.

By the end of the week, they had a basic plan drawn up and a list of materials they could afford on their modest budget. Armed with their outline, they returned to Mr. Thornton, eager to present their progress.

He listened as they explained their layered design: the outer layer would catch larger debris, the middle layer would consist of sand and gravel for added filtration, and the final layer of activated charcoal would capture impurities. They'd use a plastic container for the prototype, easy to assemble and test in the lab.

"You've done your homework," Mr. Thornton remarked, clearly impressed. "This is a solid start. Now, here's your next step: test it. Collect some water samples and start experimenting. Remember, science is as much about failure as it is about success. Don't get discouraged if things don't work out right away."

Dan nodded, the task ahead clear. "We'll start testing as soon as possible."

Brenda, however, couldn't hide her excitement. "Thank you, Mr. Thornton. This is going to be awesome—I mean, we'll make sure it's scientifically sound," she corrected herself, earning a smile from the teacher.

As they left his classroom, their minds buzzed with the possibilities. They had a plan, a project, and the beginnings of a partnership that neither had expected to be so fulfilling.

That weekend, Dan and Brenda met at Dan's house to start building their first prototype. Surrounded by piles of materials and tools, they spent hours assembling the components. With each layer they added, they talked about what could go wrong, anticipating potential issues and debating solutions.

Late into the evening, they finally had a working prototype. It was a crude, plastic-container-based model, but it held all the elements they'd planned. Brenda was the first to test it, pouring a small amount of water into the top layer. The water moved slowly through each layer, emerging slightly clearer on the other side.

They shared a silent moment of triumph, watching the water trickle out of the container.

"This is just the beginning," Dan murmured, as he realized how much more work lay ahead.

"Yeah," Brenda replied, her voice filled with quiet determination. "But it's a good start."

The journey began, with a spark of an idea and a crude prototype that held more potential than either of them could yet imagine.

Chapter 2: The Pitch

Over the weekend, Dan and Brenda refined their prototype in every way they could think of. By Sunday night, their model had gone through several adjustments: they added a more secure seal between layers to prevent leaks, tightened the cotton layer, and replaced gravel that wasn't filtering as effectively as they'd hoped. The final product was still basic, but the water it produced was noticeably clearer.

Early Monday morning, with their prototype carefully packed in a cardboard box, Dan and Brenda headed to school to present their progress to Mr. Thornton. They'd rehearsed their explanation repeatedly, anticipating any questions he might ask. Mr. Thornton wasn't the kind of teacher to let them off easy; he expected clear thinking and evidence, and they knew they'd need to be ready for a critical assessment.

As they waited outside his classroom, Brenda noticed Dan fidgeting, uncharacteristically quiet.

"You nervous?" she asked, nudging him lightly.

Dan shook his head, though his expression betrayed him. "A little. What if he thinks it's not practical enough?"

Brenda smiled. "Then he'll tell us how to make it better, like he always does. We're here to learn, right?"

Before Dan could respond, Mr. Thornton opened the door, motioning them in. "I see you both brought the prototype. Let's take a look."

Inside the classroom, they carefully set the model on his desk and unpacked it. The prototype, though modest, had a sturdy look. Dan had chosen a small plastic container with distinct layers for sand, gravel, and activated charcoal, each serving a specific filtration purpose. As they prepared to explain their design, Brenda took a deep breath, hoping Mr. Thornton would see the potential in their creation.

"Alright, walk me through it," he said, observing the prototype closely.

Dan began, his voice steady as he outlined each component's purpose. "The first layer is cotton, which we're using to trap larger particles and prevent clogging. Beneath that, we have gravel and sand for basic filtration. They'll catch smaller particles that make it through the cotton layer. And at the bottom is the activated charcoal, which absorbs impurities and enhances water clarity."

Brenda chimed in, adding, "We wanted to use materials that people can easily access and replace. If someone were to build this at home, it wouldn't cost them much, and they'd have access to cleaner water."

Mr. Thornton listened carefully, his gaze never leaving the model. After a pause, he asked, "Have you tested this? Have you compared filtered water samples to unfiltered ones?"

Brenda glanced at Dan, then nodded. "Yes, we tested a few samples. The water wasn't perfect, but it was significantly clearer. We still need to refine it, though."

Mr. Thornton leaned back, a thoughtful expression on his face. "I can see you two have put a lot of effort into this. It's a promising start, but you'll need to support your results with data. If you're serious about this project, you need to show quantitative proof that the water is safer to drink. That means taking samples to a lab, if possible, or finding a way to measure impurities yourselves."

Dan's brow furrowed. "I didn't think about lab testing. We don't have the equipment here at school. Is there any way we could arrange access to a local lab?"

Mr. Thornton tapped his fingers on his desk, thinking. "I might have some contacts who can help. There's a university nearby with a community outreach program that supports local schools. I'll see if I can get you access for testing, but no promises. In the meantime, focus on perfecting your design and preparing a clear presentation."

Brenda's eyes lit up. "Thank you, Mr. Thornton! We'll make it worth the effort, I promise."

As they left the classroom, Dan turned to Brenda, relief mingling with determination. "We've got a lot of work to do, but that went well."

Brenda grinned. "See? Told you we'd be fine. Now, let's go over what we need to tweak before any lab tests. This thing has to be as good as it can be."

Over the next few days, they threw themselves into perfecting their design, testing it with new materials and adjusting it to make the filtration as efficient as possible. Each afternoon, they met at the library or in the science lab, sifting through books on water purification, reading articles on environmental engineering, and experimenting with different combinations of materials.

One afternoon, as they worked through another test, Dan paused, staring at the water sample in front of him.

"This isn't coming out as clean as I'd hoped," he murmured. "Maybe we need to change the amount of charcoal we're using."

Brenda considered this, her gaze focused on the darkened water sample. "Or maybe we need to add an extra layer. Something to handle the smaller particles that the sand and gravel can't filter out."

The days passed in a blur of adjustments, calculations, and late-night emails. Each time they tried something new, they recorded their findings, hoping that their data would help build a compelling case for their project. They wanted not just to present a good idea but to demonstrate that it could make a measurable difference.

Finally, on a Friday afternoon, they received an email from Mr. Thornton. He'd managed to secure them an hour of lab time at the local university's water research facility the following week. For Dan and Brenda, this was the breakthrough they'd been hoping for.

"Brenda, we're actually going to test this thing in a real lab!" Dan exclaimed, barely able to contain his excitement as he read the email.

She couldn't hide her enthusiasm either. "This is huge! If the lab results confirm that it works, we'll be able to present real data. It'll give us a huge edge in the contest."

They spent the weekend refining their prototype even further, pushing to improve it before their testing slot. Every detail mattered, and they knew it. Dan focused on ensuring the model was structurally sound, while Brenda fine-tuned the layers to optimize filtration.

When Monday finally arrived, they felt as ready as they ever could. They met Mr. Thornton at the university, each carrying their supplies and samples. The lab was intimidating, filled with equipment they'd only seen in books or online, but their focus remained sharp. After a brief introduction from one of the lab technicians, they were allowed to begin testing.

The technician, a young man named Alex, watched with interest as they set up their prototype. "So, you're trying to make a portable water filtration system?"

Brenda nodded, her voice confident. "Exactly. Something people could use in areas where clean water isn't easily accessible. We want to make it simple and affordable."

Alex raised an eyebrow, impressed. "That's a tall order, but if it works, it could have a real impact. I'll help you get started with the testing."

He guided them through each step, helping them measure the impurities in their unfiltered water samples. Then, they ran the water through the prototype, watching as it slowly trickled out, clearer than it had been before. Once the filtered samples were collected, Alex ran them through the lab's analysis equipment, comparing the impurity levels before and after.

Dan and Brenda watched anxiously as he examined the results. The minutes felt like hours, and each glance he cast at the data only made them more nervous.

Finally, Alex turned to them with a smile. "You two actually pulled it off. The water isn't perfect, but the difference is measurable. Your prototype reduces impurity levels by about 60 percent, which is significant for a device made with basic materials."

Dan felt a surge of relief and excitement. "Does that mean it's viable?"

Alex nodded. "It's a strong starting point. With more refinement, you could probably improve it even further. But for a high school project, this is impressive."

They left the lab that afternoon feeling lighter than they had in weeks. Not only had they proven their idea worked, but they had data to back it up—a crucial element for the science contest. Mr. Thornton congratulated them, reminding them of the importance of clear communication and confidence in their presentation.

"Remember," he told them, "data is only half the battle. You have to convince people that this solution matters."

As they headed home, Dan and Brenda began planning their presentation, thinking through how they could best showcase their work. They brainstormed ways to explain each layer's function and convey the significance of their results. Each practiced line, every rephrased explanation, brought them closer to feeling ready.

In their final meeting before the local science contest, they practiced their pitch for Mr. Thornton, who provided feedback on everything from their posture to the phrasing of their arguments.

"You're doing great," he assured them. "Just make sure you focus on the impact this could have. It's not just about the science; it's about helping people access clean water."

The words resonated with both of them. They knew their project had grown beyond a simple classroom assignment. Now, it held the potential to be something more—something that could truly make a difference.

THE SCIENCE CONTEST

By the time they walked out of Mr. Thornton's classroom, Dan and Brenda were no longer just students with a project. They were innovators, driven by the possibility that their idea could change lives.

Chapter 3: Research and Reality Check

The week leading up to the contest found Dan and Brenda in a whirlwind of late-night research sessions, after-school meetings, and problem-solving marathons. While they had successfully built a working prototype and gathered data from the university lab, they were far from done. As they delved deeper into the science and engineering behind their project, they uncovered more complex challenges, each pushing them to rethink parts of their design.

Their first major issue was the filtration speed. Though their device managed to clean the water effectively, the flow rate was slower than they'd hoped. The filtration system took nearly five minutes to process a single cup of water—a pace that would be impractical for real-life use. This realization hit them hard during one of their lab tests.

"Five minutes for a cup?" Dan muttered, staring at the stopwatch. "At this rate, someone would need hours to filter enough water for a family."

Brenda bit her lip, considering. "We could adjust the layers, maybe? Thin them out or change the material. It might speed things up, right?"

"Maybe," Dan said thoughtfully. "But we risk losing effectiveness. If we thin out the layers, we might not catch all the impurities. We'd need to strike a balance somehow."

That evening, they returned to the library, piling stacks of books and scientific journals on the table, eager to find any hints or ideas that could lead them to a solution. Brenda poured over articles on natural filtration methods, while Dan focused on engineering journals, hunting for any techniques that could make the water flow faster without sacrificing purity.

A few hours into their research, Brenda looked up from her book, an idea forming. "I read something about gravity-fed filtration systems. They use a larger container at the top, so the force of gravity helps push the water through faster. What if we tried that? Maybe we could attach a larger reservoir to the top of our prototype."

Dan mulled it over. "That could work. We'd need a sturdy setup to support the extra weight, though. And it might make the whole system bulkier than we planned. But if it speeds up the process and keeps the water quality the same, it might be worth it."

Eager to test this new approach, they made a list of materials they'd need for the adjustment and agreed to meet at Dan's house the next afternoon to build the modified prototype.

The next day, they gathered in Dan's garage, setting up their makeshift lab on a workbench crowded with tools, containers, and scattered notes. Dan's parents were used to seeing him engrossed in projects, but even they seemed impressed by the intensity of his work with Brenda.

As they assembled the new design, Brenda brought up another challenge they'd encountered: the cost of materials. Their original goal had been to create an affordable device, but the costs of certain materials, like activated charcoal, were adding up quickly.

"Dan, I know we want this to be high-quality, but I'm worried about the price. If we're serious about making this accessible, we need to think about cheaper alternatives," Brenda said, attaching a funnel to the top reservoir.

Dan nodded, sharing her concern. "I was thinking the same thing. I've read about using homemade charcoal as a filtration medium, but it's hard to maintain the consistency of store-bought activated charcoal. We'd have to find a reliable way to make it work."

They spent the next few hours experimenting, testing different amounts of gravel, sand, and homemade charcoal. Each adjustment brought them a little closer to their goal, but progress was slow. By the time they called it a night, they had a modified prototype that seemed to filter water faster, though they still needed more tests to verify its effectiveness.

The following morning, Dan and Brenda met with Mr. Thornton, who listened intently as they explained the new changes. They showed him their updated prototype, explaining the addition of the top reservoir and the cost-cutting measures they'd tried.

Mr. Thornton inspected their model thoughtfully, occasionally nodding in approval. "You've both made excellent progress," he finally said, his expression serious but encouraging. "But I want you to keep one thing in mind as you prepare for the contest: practicality."

Brenda tilted her head, a questioning look in her eyes. "What do you mean?"

Mr. Thornton folded his hands, choosing his words carefully. "The judges will look at more than just your science. They'll want to know if your project could be useful in real-world conditions. It's one thing to show a working prototype; it's another to show them how it could be applied on a large scale."

Dan nodded slowly, the weight of Mr. Thornton's advice settling over him. "So, they'll be looking for real-world applications?"

"Exactly," Mr. Thornton replied. "Think about it—if this project were to go beyond the contest, how would people actually use it? Would it need special maintenance? Is it durable enough to work in different environments? These are the questions that'll help you refine your project even further."

Brenda and Dan exchanged a look, realizing the gravity of what lay ahead. While they'd worked hard to make their design functional, they hadn't fully considered how it would be used outside a lab environment. It was a sobering thought, one that reminded them of the complexity of creating something that could truly make a difference.

Determined to meet Mr. Thornton's challenge, they decided to add a new layer of research to their project: they would reach out to people who worked with water purification systems in real-world scenarios. Dan's mother suggested they contact the community center, where volunteers sometimes organized workshops on sustainability and community health. Brenda also knew of a local environmental group that focused on clean water initiatives.

With Mr. Thornton's support, they arranged meetings with representatives from both groups, hoping to learn more about the real-world issues surrounding water purification.

Their first meeting took place at the community center, where they met Marisol, a volunteer who had spent years working on clean water projects in rural areas. Marisol was a warm, knowledgeable woman in her thirties, with a passion for environmental education. She greeted them with a warm smile, eager to hear about their project.

After listening to their presentation, Marisol shared her experiences working in communities that lacked clean water. She explained the importance of simple, low-maintenance systems, especially in areas where access to technology or replacement parts was limited.

"Whatever you design needs to be easy to clean and repair," Marisol advised. "If it requires specialized parts or regular maintenance, people might have trouble keeping it functional over the long term."

Brenda jotted down notes as Marisol spoke, her mind buzzing with ideas. "So, simplicity and durability are key?"

"Absolutely," Marisol replied. "Also, consider where your materials are sourced. If it's too hard to find replacement parts, the whole system could become a burden rather than a help."

The next day, they met with a representative from the environmental group, who emphasized the need for cultural sensitivity when implementing new technology in unfamiliar regions. They explained that in some communities, people were hesitant to use unfamiliar devices, especially if the benefits weren't immediately clear.

"Education is essential," the representative said. "If people don't understand how the system works or why it's beneficial, they may not use it consistently. You'll need to consider that if your project goes forward."

These insights gave Dan and Brenda a renewed sense of purpose. It was clear that their project was about more than just science; it was about creating something that people could rely on, even in the toughest conditions.

Over the next few days, they incorporated these ideas into their design. Brenda suggested using locally available materials whenever possible, like gravel or sand from nearby sources, which would reduce dependency on store-bought items. Dan worked on making the model more compact, reducing the need for complex parts and focusing on ease of use.

As the deadline for the contest approached, their prototype began to take on a new shape. It was simpler, more compact, and more robust than their original design. With each improvement, they grew more confident in the potential of their project to make a real impact.

One evening, as they packed up their notes and materials after a long day of work, Dan spoke up, his voice thoughtful. "I didn't realize how much went into this. At first, it was just about making a cool filtration system, but now... it feels different."

Brenda smiled, nodding. "It's bigger than just us now. We're building something that could actually help people. That's worth all the work."

Their conversation left a lingering feeling of accomplishment. They both knew they had created something meaningful, something that went beyond a simple science project.

The night before the contest, they rehearsed their presentation one last time, each determined to showcase not just the science but the purpose behind their work. They planned to emphasize the simplicity, durability, and community-oriented aspects of their design, hoping to convey the heart of their mission.

Finally, as they packed up their materials for the big day, Brenda looked at Dan, her voice steady. "No matter what happens tomorrow, we did something important here. Whether we win or lose, we've already accomplished something we can be proud of."

Dan replied, feeling the same sense of pride. "We have. But let's make sure we do our best tomorrow. Who knows what this could turn into?"

Chapter 4: Building the Prototype

The morning sun was just starting to warm the cool autumn air as Dan and Brenda entered the school science lab. They'd been granted special access to work on their project, a privilege Mr. Thornton had arranged to support their commitment. They had spent the past week refining their research and design, consulting with experts, and now it was time to build the full prototype they'd envisioned.

As they spread out their materials on one of the long workbenches, a quiet focus settled between them. They both felt the weight of their mission—to build a durable, affordable, and effective water filtration system that could withstand real-world conditions. It was no longer just a project; it was a commitment to making a difference.

Dan was the first to break the silence. "Alright, let's get the base set up. If we start with a sturdy frame, the rest should hold up well."

Brenda nodded, already setting up the plastic container they'd chosen as the prototype's main structure. They had spent considerable time debating the ideal container shape, finally selecting a sturdy cylindrical base that could easily support the layers they intended to add.

"Let's start by securing the cotton filter at the top," Brenda said, taking a square piece of cotton and adjusting it inside the container.

Dan handed her a few small clips to hold the cotton in place, watching closely to ensure it sat evenly. They were both learning the importance of small details; one loose layer or uneven edge could throw off the filtration process entirely.

After the cotton layer, they added a thin layer of coarse gravel. Dan poured it carefully, making sure it spread evenly. Brenda followed with a finer sand layer, smoothing it over the gravel to create a tight seal. As they worked, each layer added a new dimension to their design, representing countless hours of research and refinement.

Dan stepped back, examining the setup. "We've got the basics down. Next is the activated charcoal. Let's make sure we don't use too much, or the flow rate will slow down again."

Brenda nodded, remembering the issues they'd had with earlier prototypes. She measured out a small amount of charcoal, pouring it over the sand with a steady hand. It had taken them multiple trials to perfect the balance of materials—too little charcoal, and the filtration wouldn't be effective; too much, and the water would take too long to filter.

When they finally completed the layering, Dan placed a mesh cover over the top, ensuring that nothing would shift during testing. The prototype was finished, and while it was a simple setup, they both felt a sense of pride as they looked at their creation.

Brenda couldn't help but smile. "It might not look fancy, but this thing has a lot of heart."

Dan chuckled, feeling the same quiet satisfaction. "Definitely. But let's see if it works before we get too attached."

They carefully filled the top of the container with a sample of murky water they had prepared earlier, watching as it slowly trickled through the layers. Brenda set a stopwatch, timing the process as Dan recorded notes, both eager to see the final results.

The minutes ticked by, and finally, the first drops of filtered water appeared at the bottom. It was noticeably clearer, but they knew appearances could be deceiving. Brenda held up a test strip, dipping it into the water to check for impurities. The strip didn't change color, indicating that the water was relatively clean.

Dan grinned. "I think we've got it. The test strips aren't picking up any major impurities. This is exactly what we were hoping for."

Brenda looked at him, her eyes bright. "So, we're ready to present?"

"Not yet," Dan said, his voice thoughtful. "We need to make sure it's durable. This thing can't fall apart halfway through the demonstration."

Brenda nodded, understanding his caution. "Let's try running a few more tests then. If it holds up, we'll know it's ready."

They spent the rest of the morning running test after test, making adjustments to strengthen the prototype as needed. By noon, the system was consistently producing clean water, and each test result reaffirmed their success. They'd created a prototype that was not only effective but also resilient enough to withstand repeated use.

As the contest drew closer, Dan and Brenda began practicing their presentation, determined to showcase their project with the same precision and care they'd put into building it. They knew that how they presented their idea would be just as important as the prototype itself. They needed to convey not just the science behind the project but also the purpose—their goal of helping communities in need.

Mr. Thornton had arranged for them to practice in front of a small audience, consisting of a few teachers and students who volunteered to give feedback. Though they felt prepared, standing in front of the audience made the stakes feel real.

Dan took a deep breath and began, explaining the inspiration for their project and the challenges they had overcome along the way. Brenda followed, describing the design and how each layer served a specific purpose. They spoke with a balance of technical detail and heartfelt passion, hoping their message would resonate with the audience.

When they finished, they stood silently, awaiting feedback. The teachers exchanged glances, nodding in approval, while the students seemed genuinely interested.

One teacher, Ms. Park, spoke up first. "That was very thorough, and I could tell you both believe in the purpose of this project. My only suggestion would be to simplify some of the technical explanations. Remember, not everyone will be familiar with scientific terminology."

Dan and Brenda took notes, grateful for the advice. They spent the next few days refining their script, making it as clear and accessible as possible while preserving the essence of their work. By the time the contest day arrived, they felt ready to face whatever challenges lay ahead.

The local science contest was held in the school's gymnasium, where tables lined the walls, each set up with a project representing hours of dedication and hard work. As they entered the room, Dan and Brenda felt a mix of excitement and nervousness. This was their first chance to share their project with a broader audience, and they were determined to make an impact.

They set up their display, arranging their prototype in the center of the table and surrounding it with charts, data sheets, and photographs documenting their process. Dan made sure everything was organized, while Brenda arranged their materials in a way that was both informative and inviting. They wanted their table to stand out, to draw people in and spark interest.

As the contest began, students, teachers, and judges circulated the room, stopping to ask questions and examine each project. It wasn't long before they attracted the attention of one of the judges, a tall man with glasses who introduced himself as Dr. Harvey, a retired environmental engineer.

Dr. Harvey examined their prototype closely, listening as Dan and Brenda walked him through each stage of their process. He asked pointed questions about the durability of the materials, the filtration speed, and the practicality of using the system in different environments. They answered with confidence, grateful for the hours they'd spent preparing.

"Impressive," Dr. Harvey said, looking genuinely pleased. "You two have put a lot of thought into this. And I appreciate the focus on accessibility and cost-effectiveness. Often, projects like this get lost in complexity, but you've kept it grounded."

His praise gave them a surge of confidence, but the real test came when the next judge, a stern woman named Ms. Larkin, arrived at their table. She scrutinized their prototype with a critical eye, asking challenging questions about their methodology and the limitations of their design.

"What would happen if this device was exposed to extreme weather conditions?" she asked, her tone sharp. "Could it still function effectively?"

Dan paused, caught off guard. They hadn't tested it under extreme conditions, but he answered honestly. "We haven't tested it for extreme weather yet, but we're open to exploring ways to make it more weather-resistant in the future."

Ms. Larkin nodded, seemingly satisfied with his honesty. "It's a strong foundation, but remember that real-world applications often come with unexpected challenges. If you move forward with this, think about how you can adapt the design to make it even more resilient."

As Ms. Larkin moved on, Brenda exhaled, relieved. "That was intense. But I think we did okay."

Dan nodded, feeling a surge of pride. "We held our own. No matter what happens, I think we did our best."

They continued presenting to students, teachers, and curious onlookers throughout the day, each interaction reinforcing their confidence. By the end of the contest, they were exhausted but filled with a deep sense of accomplishment. They'd shared their vision, answered challenging questions, and seen people's genuine interest in their work.

When the judges finally announced the winners, Dan and Brenda held their breath. They knew the competition was tough, but they hoped their project would stand out for its purpose and practicality.

"We are pleased to announce the first-place winner for the local science contest," the announcer began, "an innovative project focused on creating a sustainable, affordable water filtration system. Congratulations to Dan Carter and Brenda Collins!"

A rush of excitement washed over them as they shook hands with the judges and accepted their award. For the first time, their hard work had been recognized not just by their teacher or classmates, but by professionals who saw the potential in their idea. They felt a new sense of validation and purpose, knowing they were one step closer to making a real difference.

Chapter 5: Entering the Contest

After their triumph at the local contest, Dan and Brenda barely had time to celebrate before they were thrust back into planning mode. Winning had come with a thrilling new responsibility—the opportunity to compete at the regional level. This was a bigger stage, with tougher competition and more eyes on their project. The realization filled them with equal parts excitement and anxiety.

As they poured over their data, refining their presentation, a new pressure emerged: making their prototype not only functional but also competitive enough to stand out among other advanced projects. They knew that every team entering the regional level would be bringing their best ideas, and their simple filtration system, while effective, would need an extra edge to captivate the judges.

One afternoon after school, Dan and Brenda met in the library, where they had set up a small work station with a binder full of notes, test results, and the diagrams of their latest prototype. Dan flipped through their recent feedback from Mr. Thornton, which included a note about durability and efficiency.

"We need to go deeper with our testing," Dan said, tapping a finger on one of Mr. Thornton's notes. "There's still some room for improvement with the flow rate and durability."

Brenda nodded, a determined glint in her eye. "Agreed. And we should also add some visual aids to our presentation. At regionals, people might not understand the impact just from looking at the prototype. They'll need to see what it can do."

"I was thinking the same thing," Dan replied. "If we add some before-and-after photos of the water samples, it'll be easier to see the filtration power. And we could even create a small video showing the water going through the layers."

The idea was ambitious, but Brenda's eyes brightened with excitement. "Yes! That's exactly what we need. The visuals could make a huge difference. Let's make a list of the shots we need for the video."

As they discussed angles, lighting, and shot lists, they noticed another student lingering nearby, her gaze fixed on their workstation. She was tall, with a confident stance and an intense focus that immediately set her apart. Dan recognized her immediately—Sydney Lane, a well-known competitor from a neighboring high school who was rumored to have won nearly every science competition in the region.

Sydney approached their table, her expression polite but assessing. "Nice setup you've got there," she said, glancing at the binder filled with neatly labeled tabs.

Dan looked up, slightly surprised. "Oh, thanks. We're getting ready for regionals."

Brenda offered a friendly smile. "Are you competing too?"

Sydney nodded, a small, enigmatic smile on her face. "Yep. My team's working on an automated soil nutrient analyzer. It's designed to help farmers monitor their soil's nutrient levels remotely. We're hoping it'll have a big impact in areas where soil degradation is a problem."

Dan exchanged a look with Brenda, both impressed by the sophistication of her project. The concept was advanced, both in its application and technical requirements. The soil analyzer sounded like a well-funded, high-tech project—one that had been developed with resources beyond what they had at their disposal.

"That sounds impressive," Dan said, unable to hide a trace of admiration.

Sydney shrugged, a flicker of pride in her expression. "It's been challenging, but worth it. These competitions are about pushing boundaries, right?"

Brenda nodded, feeling a subtle surge of competitiveness. "Absolutely. We're working on making clean water more accessible. Our project focuses on developing a low-cost water filtration system."

Sydney's gaze shifted to their prototype, her eyes narrowing thoughtfully. "Interesting. I've read about filtration systems like that. They're not easy to get right, especially on a budget."

Dan noticed her tone—both appreciative and competitive. There was no question that Sydney viewed them as serious competitors. He straightened his posture, matching her energy. "We've had a few challenges, but we're committed to making it work."

Sydney nodded, her expression softening slightly. "Well, I'll see you both at regionals. Good luck."

With that, she walked away, leaving Dan and Brenda feeling both inspired and slightly nervous.

Brenda glanced at Dan, her voice dropping to a whisper. "I didn't expect her project to be so advanced. That nutrient analyzer sounds high-tech."

Dan sighed, his mind racing with thoughts. "Yeah, but that doesn't change our goal. Our project is still valuable. We just need to focus on making it as strong as possible. Let's double down and make sure we're ready."

They both agreed to up their game, working late into the evening over the next week, recording footage of their prototype in action, taking detailed water samples, and creating a visual representation of the filtration process. They tested the model under various conditions—adding sediment to simulate river water, using samples with different levels of contamination, and timing the results to improve flow rates. Each test brought them a new insight, which they added to their presentation in the form of data points and comparison graphs.

The night before the regional contest, they met at Brenda's house to run through their presentation. They practiced every line, anticipating potential questions and rehearsing their answers until each response felt natural. Brenda's living room was transformed into a temporary stage, with posters on easels, a makeshift projector for their video, and the prototype displayed on a small table.

By midnight, they were both exhausted but feeling prepared.

"We've done all we can," Brenda said, collapsing onto the couch, her voice barely a whisper. "Tomorrow, we just have to show them what we've built."

Dan nodded, his own exhaustion visible but tempered by a quiet confidence. "Whatever happens, we've worked hard. Let's focus on sharing what we've created."

The next morning, the regional contest venue buzzed with energy as students from different schools set up their projects. Each table represented months of hard work, and the variety of topics was astounding—everything from robotics and genetics to environmental sustainability. Dan and Brenda's table was positioned near the middle of the room, and they set up their display with meticulous care, placing their prototype in the center and arranging the posters and video screen around it.

As they finished setting up, they noticed Sydney at a nearby table, surrounded by her team and an impressive array of equipment. Her setup looked polished and professional, with sleek posters and technical diagrams. Despite the friendly conversation they'd had earlier, Sydney's demeanor was now fully focused, her gaze set on her project with a fierce intensity.

Dan glanced at Brenda, sharing an unspoken understanding. They both knew they were up against some formidable competition, but they were here to give it their best shot.

As the event began, judges started circulating the room, evaluating each project in detail. It didn't take long for a panel of three judges to arrive at Dan and Brenda's table, their expressions attentive and curious. The lead judge, a middle-aged woman with sharp eyes and a warm smile, introduced herself as Dr. Morales, an environmental science professor.

"Good morning, Dan and Brenda," she began, scanning their setup with interest. "We're excited to learn about your project. Please take us through it."

Dan and Brenda launched into their presentation, starting with the initial inspiration for their project—the need for affordable, accessible clean water. They explained the limitations of current filtration systems and how their design offered a low-cost alternative. Brenda pointed to the prototype, demonstrating each layer of filtration and how the materials were carefully chosen to maximize efficiency while keeping costs down.

As they spoke, Dr. Morales nodded thoughtfully, clearly intrigued. "I appreciate the practical approach you've taken. Water filtration is a complex issue, and accessibility is often overlooked. Tell me, how would this design hold up under more challenging conditions, like natural disasters or locations without consistent water sources?"

Dan took a deep breath, prepared for this question. "Our design is modular and easy to repair, so even if parts were damaged, they could be replaced with locally available materials. We're also working on a more robust frame for areas with extreme weather conditions. It's still a work in progress, but our goal is to make it as resilient as possible."

Dr. Morales exchanged a look with her fellow judges, who seemed equally impressed. The next judge, a man with a background in engineering, asked them about the science behind their material choices, focusing on how they balanced cost and effectiveness. Dan handled the technical questions, explaining the filtration mechanics, while Brenda described their commitment to sustainability and simplicity.

The third judge, a representative from a nonprofit organization focused on community health, asked about the social impact of their project. "How do you see this design being used in communities that might not have the infrastructure for maintenance or distribution?"

Brenda's voice softened, her passion clear. "Our hope is that local community leaders could be trained to build and maintain these systems themselves. We've tried to make the design as intuitive as possible, so even without advanced tools, people could learn to use and repair it."

The judge smiled, visibly moved. "Thank you for sharing that. It's a thoughtful approach."

When the judges moved on, Dan and Brenda felt a wave of relief and pride. Their presentation had gone smoothly, and it was clear the judges saw potential in their work. As the day wore on, they watched other presentations, learning from the diverse approaches their peers had taken. Sydney's project drew a large crowd, and her soil nutrient analyzer was undeniably impressive, but Dan and Brenda felt a quiet confidence in their own work.

Finally, as the contest came to a close, all participants gathered for the awards ceremony. The anticipation in the room was palpable as the announcer began listing the winners for each category.

When the announcer reached the "Environmental Impact" category, Dan and Brenda held their breath. This was their category—the one that represented their purpose and goal.

"We're thrilled to present the award for Environmental Impact to a project that demonstrates both practicality and potential for real-world change. Congratulations to Dan Carter and Brenda Collins for their water filtration system."

Cheers erupted around them as they made their way to the stage, accepting their award with wide smiles and grateful hearts. The judges had recognized not only the science behind their project but the deeper impact they hoped to achieve.

Chapter 6: The Local Contest

The news of their victory at the regional level spread quickly throughout the school. Students they barely knew congratulated them in the hallways, and Mr. Thornton organized a small celebration in the science lab with cupcakes and sparkling apple juice. The excitement only fueled their determination; the nationals were now within reach, and they were more committed than ever to refining their project.

Over the next few days, Dan and Brenda returned to their regular routine, but their minds were consumed by ideas to improve their filtration system. They understood that nationals would attract the best of the best, with projects far more advanced and well-funded than what they had encountered so far. If they wanted to stand out, they'd need to focus on making their project not only effective but groundbreaking.

One afternoon, they met in the school library to brainstorm. Brenda spread out their notes and schematics across the table, organizing everything by section: filtration methods, community impact, and scalability.

"So," she said, scanning their notes, "we know our filtration works for small amounts of water, but what about larger quantities? What if we designed a scaled-up model, something that could handle more than just a few cups at a time?"

Dan leaned back, considering her idea. "That's a good point. If we could show that it works on a larger scale, it would make a bigger impact, especially in areas where people need more than just a few liters of water each day."

"Exactly," Brenda replied. "I was thinking we could use larger layers of filtration material, maybe a bigger container. If we increase the volume but keep the basic design, it should still work—at least in theory."

They began sketching ideas for a larger prototype, debating materials, dimensions, and potential challenges. As they worked, Dan made a list of the additional materials they'd need and the adjustments required to ensure their design remained cost-effective.

The next day, they met in the science lab with Mr. Thornton, who watched their preparations with a mixture of pride and curiosity.

"I see you're both diving into the details again," he said, glancing at their expanding list of materials. "What's the new plan?"

Brenda explained their goal to create a larger-scale model, detailing their design and the reasons behind it. Mr. Thornton listened carefully, then offered his own insights.

"You'll need to consider water pressure and flow rate on a larger scale," he suggested. "If the water moves too slowly, it could affect the filtration efficiency, but if it moves too quickly, impurities might slip through. Balancing those factors will be key."

Dan jotted down Mr. Thornton's feedback, grateful for the guidance. "We'll run some tests to measure the pressure and adjust the materials as needed."

They spent the next few days building their scaled-up prototype, experimenting with different materials and configurations. Each test brought new challenges—some layers proved too thick, causing the water to slow down significantly, while others weren't dense enough to filter effectively. It was a painstaking process, but with each adjustment, they came closer to a working model.

Finally, after several late nights and numerous trial runs, they had a larger prototype that filtered water at a faster rate while maintaining purity. The scaled-up design felt like a major breakthrough, and with the national contest drawing closer, they knew they were ready to present something remarkable.

On the morning of the national contest, the school's science lab buzzed with excitement as Dan and Brenda gathered their materials for the event. Mr. Thornton arrived early to help them load the prototype into his car, offering them last-minute advice on presentation and handling questions from the judges.

As they drove to the contest venue, Brenda gazed out the window, absorbing the significance of the moment. This was the culmination of months of work, trial and error, and late nights spent poring over data. She looked over at Dan, feeling a renewed sense of partnership in their shared journey.

When they arrived at the venue—a large conference hall bustling with students from across the country—they took a moment to appreciate the scale of the event. Rows of tables were set up, each filled with ambitious projects ranging from robotics to biochemistry to environmental science. The level of sophistication was undeniable, and both felt the gravity of the competition they were up against.

Dan set up their table meticulously, arranging their prototype, data charts, and before-and-after water samples. Brenda organized their presentation materials and practiced explaining the process one last time under her breath, ensuring every detail was in place. By the time they were finished, their setup looked polished, each piece reflecting their hard work and dedication.

As the event began, they observed the judges making their rounds, moving from project to project with thoughtful expressions and serious inquiries. When the judges approached their table, Dan and Brenda prepared themselves, ready to share the story behind their work.

One of the judges, a professor from a well-known university, examined their prototype closely, nodding as Dan explained each layer's purpose and the unique challenges they had overcome. Brenda followed, detailing the cost-saving aspects of their design and the potential impact for communities lacking access to clean water.

The professor raised a question, his expression intrigued. "This is impressive work. But tell me, how would you adapt this design for varying water sources? For instance, water from a river may have different contaminants compared to water from a well."

Dan considered his answer carefully. "That's a great question. We designed the system to be flexible, so it could be customized depending on the type of water source. For heavily contaminated sources, we could add more activated charcoal or include an extra sand layer. For cleaner sources, the layers could be reduced to speed up the filtration process."

The judge nodded approvingly, seemingly satisfied. The other judges asked additional questions, probing deeper into their methodology and the practical applications of their design. Each answer they gave felt like a small victory, a testament to the hours they had spent preparing and refining their project.

After their presentation, the judges moved on, leaving Dan and Brenda to absorb the rush of relief and excitement. They had given their best, answering each question with clarity and purpose. Now, all they could do was wait.

The hours passed in a blur of conversations, presentations, and glimpses of other projects. They met students from all over the country, each passionate about their work, each project reflecting a unique blend of innovation and dedication. Brenda found herself captivated by a project involving biodegradable plastics, while Dan was drawn to a team working on a solar-powered desalination system. The level of talent around them was humbling, yet inspiring.

When the awards ceremony finally began, everyone gathered around the stage, the atmosphere charged with anticipation. The announcer listed each category, presenting awards for the most innovative projects, the best applications in environmental science, and the strongest presentations.

Finally, the announcer reached their category—Social and Environmental Impact.

"This year's award for Social and Environmental Impact goes to a project that combines scientific rigor with a profound sense of social responsibility," the announcer said, pausing for dramatic effect. "Congratulations to Dan Carter and Brenda Collins for their water filtration system!"

The sound of applause filled the room as Dan and Brenda made their way to the stage, their hearts pounding with disbelief and excitement. Receiving the award was surreal; they had dreamed of this moment, but to experience it in reality felt overwhelming. As they accepted their trophy and shook hands with the judges, the weight of their journey settled over them—a journey defined by perseverance, creativity, and a shared purpose.

Chapter 7: Going Regional

Returning home as national contest winners filled Dan and Brenda with a new sense of possibility. Their hard work had earned them recognition, but their victory also came with heightened expectations. Their water filtration system had attracted local attention, from the school principal to members of the town council, all eager to learn more about how two high school students had created a solution with so much potential.

A few days after returning, Mr. Thornton called them both into his classroom after school. The excitement in his voice was unmistakable.

"I have news for you both," he began, gesturing for them to take a seat. "I spoke with some people in the town's environmental committee, and they're very interested in your project. They'd like to invite you to present it at the upcoming regional environmental fair."

Dan and Brenda exchanged a look, both thrilled and a little daunted. The regional environmental fair was a public event where projects weren't just evaluated by a panel of judges but also displayed to a wide audience, including scientists, environmental advocates, and potential investors. It would be an invaluable opportunity to show the impact their project could have, but it would also bring them face-to-face with experienced professionals in the field.

"Presenting at the fair could open a lot of doors for you," Mr. Thornton continued. "You might even meet people who could help take your project to the next level. But," he added, his tone serious, "it'll mean more work. You'll need to refine your prototype even further and prepare for questions from people who know this field well."

Dan took a deep breath, mentally cataloging the changes they could make. "We'll need to run more rigorous tests and gather additional data. If we're presenting to environmental experts, we'll need to be able to defend every aspect of the design."

Brenda nodded in agreement, already brimming with ideas. "I think we should also focus on scalability—showing how our design could be adapted to different community needs and environments."

"Exactly," Mr. Thornton said with a smile. "You two have a strong foundation. Now, it's about taking that next step. I'll be here to help you along the way."

As they left his classroom, Dan and Brenda discussed their plan of action, realizing the fair was only three weeks away. It would be a tight timeline, but they were determined to make the most of this opportunity.

For the next few days, they threw themselves into research, revisiting the design and gathering as much information as possible. They tested the prototype under different conditions, simulating real-life challenges such as heavy contamination, temperature changes, and long-term use. They analyzed each result, documenting everything in meticulous detail to ensure their data was both thorough and compelling.

One afternoon, as they were reviewing their notes in the school library, Brenda looked up thoughtfully.

"You know," she said, "we haven't really explored the idea of community involvement. If we're talking about deploying this system in different regions, it can't just be about the science. It has to be something that people can connect with and understand. I think we need to consider an educational aspect."

Dan raised an eyebrow. "Educational? Like training people on how to use it?"

"Not just that," Brenda replied. "Think about it—clean water is essential, but so is understanding why filtration matters and how they can maintain the system. If we involve local communities in the process, teaching them not just how the system works but why it's effective, then it becomes more than just a tool. It becomes something they feel ownership over."

Dan considered this, realizing the depth of her insight. "That's actually a great idea. We could include a simple guide or even a short workshop model for communities using the system. It would give them control over the maintenance and troubleshooting."

Excited by the new direction, they began outlining ways to make their project more community-oriented. Brenda suggested creating a visual guide—something with clear illustrations to show how each layer of filtration worked and how to assemble and clean the device. Dan proposed making it accessible in multiple languages, an addition that would make it easier for people from diverse backgrounds to understand and use.

Their project was growing beyond a mere prototype; it was becoming a multi-faceted solution designed not only to provide clean water but to empower those who used it.

As the day of the fair approached, they faced one final hurdle: funding. To build a second prototype, create the visual materials, and develop training guides, they would need more resources than they had initially anticipated. It was a reality check, a reminder that great ideas often required more than just passion and hard work.

Unsure where to turn, they met with Mr. Thornton to discuss their options.

"Well," he said, considering their situation, "we don't have much funding through the school, but there are a few grants available for students working on environmental projects. I can help you apply for one, but it might not come through in time for the fair."

Dan sighed, feeling the weight of the financial challenge. "So we'd have to make do with what we have?"

Mr. Thornton smiled, a glint of optimism in his eyes. "Not necessarily. There's one more option—crowdfunding. If you're open to sharing your project online, you could set up a page where people can support your work. It might be enough to cover the essentials."

Brenda's face lit up. "That's a great idea! We could create a short video explaining our project and why it's important. People might be more willing to help if they understand the impact it could have."

With Mr. Thornton's help, they set up a crowdfunding page, filming a heartfelt video that introduced their project and outlined their goals. They explained the importance of clean water, the unique aspects of their filtration system, and how even a small contribution could help bring their vision to life.

To their surprise, support began pouring in almost immediately. Friends, family members, and even a few strangers donated to their cause, leaving encouraging comments that motivated them to keep pushing forward. Within a week, they had raised enough to cover their costs, and they used the funds to purchase high-quality materials and print professional training guides for their presentation.

The day of the regional environmental fair dawned bright and clear. Arriving early, they set up their booth with a sense of excitement and purpose. Their table was meticulously organized, showcasing their prototype, training materials, and visual aids. A small monitor looped the crowdfunding video, providing context to anyone passing by.

As the fair opened to the public, Dan and Brenda quickly drew a crowd. People were intrigued by the simplicity of their design and its potential impact, and as they explained each layer of filtration, they could see the recognition in people's eyes. Their project wasn't just an abstract concept; it was something tangible, something that people could imagine using in real-life scenarios.

One of the fair's attendees, a woman named Emma who worked for a non-profit organization focused on clean water initiatives, stopped by their booth. She listened intently as they presented their prototype and training guides, visibly impressed.

"This is exactly the kind of grassroots solution we need," Emma said, her voice filled with enthusiasm. "I work with communities in remote areas, and we often struggle to find affordable, reliable filtration options. Your project could be incredibly beneficial."

Brenda's excitement grew as Emma asked more questions, each one delving deeper into the potential of their system. Emma mentioned that her organization was always looking for projects that could be piloted in local communities and hinted that they might be interested in partnering with Dan and Brenda.

After Emma moved on, Dan turned to Brenda, a gleam of excitement in his eyes. "If we get a partnership like that, our project could actually make it out into the world. This could be our chance."

They continued presenting to a steady stream of attendees, each conversation reinforcing the impact of their work. They met researchers, community leaders, and students, each intrigued by their filtration system and eager to learn more. Some even took photos of their prototype and training guides, asking if they could share the project with colleagues.

At the end of the day, an awards ceremony was held to recognize standout projects. Though Dan and Brenda were hopeful, they tried not to dwell on the outcome, knowing that simply participating had been a valuable experience. But as the announcer listed the top projects, their names were called as the winners of the "Community Impact" award.

Walking up to the stage, they accepted the award with a mixture of pride and gratitude, their hearts full with the knowledge that their work had resonated with others. The recognition felt like validation, not only of their scientific efforts but of the deeper purpose behind their project.

Chapter 8: Unexpected Setbacks

After their success at the regional fair, Dan and Brenda felt like they were on top of the world. Their project had earned both local praise and the interest of several organizations, including Emma's nonprofit focused on clean water access. Everything seemed to be falling into place, and the dream of bringing their water filtration system to real communities was closer than ever.

However, as they moved forward, they quickly realized that scaling a project from a high school science fair prototype to a functioning model for widespread use was more challenging than they had anticipated. Each new step revealed issues they hadn't foreseen, and the enthusiasm that had once driven their efforts now faced a series of unexpected setbacks.

The first challenge hit when they tried to build additional prototypes. While they had raised some funds through their crowdfunding campaign, the cost of materials began to add up quickly. The scaled-up prototypes required more of everything—activated charcoal, gravel, sand, and even the plastic containers. Shipping costs for the materials were higher than they'd budgeted, and they found themselves stretching every dollar just to complete each model.

One evening, after a long day of work in the school's science lab, Dan sat down with Brenda, looking over their dwindling funds with a growing sense of worry.

"We're running low on resources," he said, his voice filled with frustration. "At this rate, we're barely going to make it through these prototypes, let alone create models for testing in real communities."

Brenda looked thoughtful, though her expression mirrored Dan's concern. "Maybe we could switch to alternative materials—something we can source locally. It might make the prototypes less costly to produce."

Dan considered her suggestion. "That could work, but we'd have to test each new material to make sure it's just as effective. If we compromise on quality, the whole project loses its purpose."

They agreed to try sourcing materials from local suppliers, hoping to reduce their expenses. However, finding consistent quality for items like sand and gravel proved difficult, and they spent countless hours testing each new batch. The variations impacted the filtration system's effectiveness, forcing them to constantly adjust the setup. Despite their best efforts, the quality wasn't always reliable, and they worried how these inconsistencies might affect the project's long-term feasibility.

Just as they were beginning to get a handle on the material costs, they encountered their next obstacle: testing their prototypes in real-world conditions. Emma's nonprofit had arranged for them to send one of their models to a rural community for initial testing, but they soon discovered that the setup and maintenance required a level of expertise that was hard to communicate remotely.

The first feedback from the field was mixed. While the filtration system worked, the locals reported that the flow rate was slower than expected, and they weren't sure how to replace the filtering materials once they were used up. Dan and Brenda hadn't considered how difficult it would be to provide remote support, and the realization that their design might not be as user-friendly as they'd thought left them feeling frustrated.

One day, after reading through another round of feedback, Brenda slumped in her chair, her expression defeated. "We thought this was supposed to be easy for anyone to use, but it sounds like we've made it too complicated."

Dan ran a hand through his hair, sharing her discouragement. "We've spent so much time perfecting the design, but maybe we were too focused on the science and not enough on the usability. We can't expect people to just figure out all the details on their own."

The experience was a humbling reminder that creating an effective system wasn't just about the science; it was about making sure people could actually use it. They realized that if they wanted their system to work in a wide range of conditions, they'd need to make the design simpler, more intuitive, and adaptable.

Determined to address these issues, they brainstormed ways to improve the user experience. They decided to create a more detailed user manual, one that included step-by-step illustrations and straightforward language. They also considered ways to color-code the layers of the filtration system so that users would know exactly where each material went without needing complex instructions.

For the next few days, they worked late into the evening, creating diagrams and refining the language in the user guide to make it as accessible as possible. Brenda took charge of the illustrations, sketching out each step with simple visuals that could be understood even by those unfamiliar with water filtration.

"This might be our best chance to make the system work," Brenda said, examining her latest sketch. "If people can understand the setup easily, it'll be one less barrier for them to use it effectively."

Dan agreed, feeling a renewed sense of purpose. "And if we're successful with this community test, it could prove that our design has real potential for widespread use."

Despite their preparations, however, the setbacks continued. A few days before their first scheduled field test, Dan received an email from Emma, informing them that the nonprofit was facing funding cuts. The cuts meant that their field testing program would be delayed indefinitely, and for now, their support for Dan and Brenda's project would have to be put on hold.

The news was a heavy blow. The nonprofit had been their biggest supporter, and without their backing, Dan and Brenda felt as though they were stranded. They had poured so much of their time and resources into preparing for the field test, and now it seemed like all their work was unraveling.

Brenda paced the lab, her frustration barely contained. "We were so close. Everything was set, and now... it's like we're back to square one."

Dan shared her disappointment, but he tried to stay optimistic. "Maybe this is just a temporary setback. We can still keep working, testing locally. It doesn't have to be the end."

Despite his words, both of them felt the discouragement settling in. They had worked so hard, overcome so many obstacles, and yet it seemed as though their project was slipping out of their control. As the days passed, they found it difficult to muster the same enthusiasm that had once driven their efforts.

One afternoon, Mr. Thornton called them into his classroom, sensing their frustration. He'd noticed the change in their attitude, and he wanted to help them find a way forward.

"I know things haven't been easy," he said, his tone understanding. "But you've come too far to let a few setbacks stop you. Think about why you started this project in the first place. The goal was always to make a difference, and you're still closer to that goal than most people ever get."

Brenda sighed, her voice heavy. "It just feels like every time we make progress, something else goes wrong. It's hard to stay motivated when we're facing so many roadblocks."

Mr. Thornton gave them a thoughtful look. "I understand. But remember, every great project faces obstacles. Sometimes it's the setbacks that teach us the most valuable lessons. Instead of seeing these as failures, think of them as opportunities to refine and strengthen your design."

Dan felt a glimmer of hope in Mr. Thornton's words. "So you're saying we should keep going, even if it feels like everything's against us?"

"Exactly," Mr. Thornton replied. "Resilience is as important as innovation. You've shown that you can create something meaningful, but now it's time to show that you have the persistence to see it through."

His words reignited their determination, and they left the meeting with a renewed commitment to their project. They decided to regroup, taking a step back to assess what was working and what needed improvement. The experience had taught them that sometimes, progress required patience and flexibility, even in the face of setbacks.

Over the next few weeks, they focused on the areas that they could control. They continued testing their prototypes locally, making adjustments to improve the flow rate and durability. They reached out to a few small businesses for additional funding, hoping to secure enough resources to keep their project alive. It was slow, challenging work, but each small victory reminded them of their goal and kept them moving forward.

Chapter 9: The Regional Contest

As the weeks passed, Dan and Brenda pushed through the challenges with a renewed sense of commitment. They had survived the setbacks, adapted their design, and learned to think creatively to keep their project alive. Now, with their revised prototype and updated training materials, they were ready for the regional science contest, a competition that would bring together the top high school projects from across the state.

The contest was held in a large convention center, bustling with students, teachers, and judges. Each team had a designated booth where they could showcase their project, and the entire setup looked more like a professional trade show than a high school science fair. The scale of the event was intimidating, but Dan and Brenda were determined to make their project stand out.

Their booth was carefully organized. In the center, they placed their newest prototype—sleek and sturdy, with each layer clearly labeled to demonstrate the filtration process. Behind it, they set up a poster board with detailed diagrams, data charts, and a before-and-after display of water samples. They even included a tablet that looped a short video explaining their journey, from initial idea to prototype development, along with testimonials from people who had tested the filtration system.

As they finished setting up, Brenda looked around at the other booths. Some teams had projects that looked highly technical, involving robotics, genetic engineering, and advanced coding. Next to these high-tech projects, their filtration system seemed deceptively simple, but Dan reminded her that simplicity was one of their project's strengths.

"This contest is about impact, not just complexity," he said, sensing her doubts. "Our goal was always to create something that anyone could use, something practical and accessible. That's what makes our project special."

Brenda took a deep breath, allowing his words to reassure her. "You're right. This project means something. And we know it works."

As the contest began, the judges started moving from booth to booth, examining each project closely. Dan and Brenda watched as judges engaged with other students, asking questions and scrutinizing every detail. When the judges finally approached their booth, Dan and Brenda braced themselves, ready to present their project with clarity and confidence.

The head judge, Dr. Rivera, introduced himself. He was a tall man with an air of authority, his sharp gaze indicating that he didn't miss a thing. Two other judges accompanied him—a woman named Dr. Ellis, who specialized in environmental science, and Mr. Harris, a former engineer turned science educator.

"Good afternoon," Dr. Rivera said, scanning their booth with interest. "Tell us about your project."

Brenda began the presentation, explaining the inspiration behind their design. She described the need for affordable, accessible water filtration in areas without reliable access to clean water. Dan followed, detailing the science behind each layer of the system and how it effectively filtered out impurities.

As they spoke, the judges listened attentively, occasionally jotting down notes. Dr. Ellis asked about the materials they used and how they ensured each layer was effective.

"We tested different materials for each layer to find the best combination of cost and efficiency," Dan explained. "The cotton layer traps larger particles, while the sand and gravel layers catch smaller impurities. The activated charcoal at the bottom absorbs remaining contaminants, improving both the clarity and safety of the water."

Dr. Ellis nodded, clearly interested. "Impressive. How did you handle issues of durability? In real-world applications, these filters would need to last over time, possibly under rough conditions."

Brenda took over, describing the adjustments they'd made to strengthen the design. "We've reinforced the container to prevent leaks, and we created a user manual with clear, simple instructions for maintenance and replacement. Our goal was to make it as user-friendly as possible, so people wouldn't need any special tools or expertise to keep it working."

The judges seemed satisfied with their answers, but Mr. Harris posed another challenging question. "What about scalability? Let's say a small community wanted to use this system. Could it be adapted to handle larger volumes of water?"

Dan explained how their design could be scaled up with larger containers and thicker filtration layers, all while preserving the same fundamental principles. "We've even started working on a larger prototype, which can handle higher volumes without sacrificing filtration quality. It's still in development, but it's something we're actively exploring."

Dr. Rivera looked impressed, his gaze shifting from the prototype to the video looping on their tablet. "It seems like you've thought through a lot of potential challenges. I appreciate the practical approach. Often, simple solutions are the ones that make the biggest difference."

After asking a few more questions, the judges thanked them and moved on to the next booth. Dan and Brenda exchanged a look of relief and excitement—they had done it. They had answered every question with confidence, and the judges seemed genuinely impressed.

The rest of the day was a blur of conversations and presentations. Fellow students, teachers, and even members of the public came by to learn about their project. They met students working on fascinating projects, from climate models to renewable energy devices, each one showcasing the depth of talent and creativity in the room. But throughout it all, Dan and Brenda kept coming back to the simplicity and purpose of their own project, feeling a renewed pride in the journey that had brought them here.

They were particularly touched by one interaction with a teacher from another school who stopped by their booth. She listened to their presentation with intense interest and, after a few questions, shared her own experiences.

"I grew up in a rural area where clean water was a luxury," she said, her voice quiet but filled with emotion. "Seeing young people work on solutions like this—it's powerful. This project could truly make a difference in communities like the one I came from. Thank you."

Her words resonated with both of them, reminding them why they had started this journey. It wasn't just about winning a contest; it was about creating something meaningful, something that could improve lives in real ways.

When the time came for the awards ceremony, everyone gathered around the stage, the atmosphere buzzing with anticipation. Dan and Brenda knew they had done their best, but the competition was fierce, and they couldn't be certain how their project would stack up against the others.

The announcer began listing the awards, starting with categories like "Best Use of Technology" and "Most Innovative Design." They applauded for each winner, feeling both excited for their peers and anxious about the results of their own category.

Finally, the announcer reached the category they had been waiting for: "Best Social and Environmental Impact."

"This award recognizes a project that addresses pressing social and environmental challenges with a practical, accessible solution," the announcer said. "Our winners demonstrated not only scientific rigor but also a commitment to positive change in their communities."

Dan and Brenda held their breath, feeling their hearts race.

"The award for Best Social and Environmental Impact goes to... Dan Carter and Brenda Collins for their water filtration system!"

The room filled with applause as Dan and Brenda made their way to the stage, both of them feeling a mix of excitement, pride, and relief. As they accepted the award, they felt the weight of the journey they had taken together, each setback and triumph culminating in this moment.

On stage, the announcer invited them to say a few words. Dan took a deep breath, looking out at the audience, and spoke from the heart.

"When we started this project, our goal was to make clean water more accessible, especially for communities where it's hard to come by. We faced a lot of challenges along the way, but each one taught us something valuable. Winning this award means so much to us, but what matters most is knowing that our work might help people in need. Thank you to everyone who supported us."

Brenda followed, her voice filled with gratitude. "We couldn't have done this without our teacher, Mr. Thornton, and all the people who believed in us along the way. This award is as much for them as it is for us. Thank you."

As they left the stage, they felt a profound sense of accomplishment. The award was a testament to their hard work and resilience, a recognition of everything they had overcome to reach this point.

Chapter 10: Preparing for Nationals

The excitement from winning the Best Social and Environmental Impact award lingered long after the regional contest. The experience had strengthened Dan and Brenda's resolve, and the recognition gave them new confidence in their work. But they knew that their journey was far from over. Winning at regionals meant they had qualified for the nationals, a level of competition that would demand more refinement, creativity, and preparation than ever before.

The national science contest was set to be the largest event they'd ever participated in. Teams from across the country would showcase groundbreaking projects, many with significant backing from sponsors, universities, and research institutions. Dan and Brenda were aware that they'd be up against some of the most advanced high school projects in the country, and if they wanted to stand out, they would have to bring their very best.

One afternoon, they sat down with Mr. Thornton in his classroom to map out their plan. The sun cast a warm glow across the room, and their teacher's encouraging smile gave them a sense of reassurance as they discussed their next steps.

"You've already accomplished so much," Mr. Thornton began, his tone proud. "But nationals will push you even further. The judges will be looking at every aspect of your project—its technical foundation, innovation, and societal impact. You'll need to prepare for more in-depth questions and present your data with absolute clarity."

Dan glanced at Brenda, feeling the weight of their task. "We're ready to put in the work, Mr. Thornton. We just need to figure out how to make our project stand out against such stiff competition."

Mr. Thornton considered this, then leaned forward. "Your project's strength lies in its practicality and accessibility. Many of the other teams might have more complex designs, but what you've created has real-world impact. Emphasize that. Think about how you can refine the prototype to make it even more resilient and user-friendly, and focus on sharing stories about how it could help communities."

Brenda's eyes lit up with a new idea. "What if we included testimonials from people who've used our prototype or supported our project? We could ask some of the people we've talked to for quotes about the importance of clean water and how our system could help. It would make the presentation more personal."

Dan nodded, catching onto the idea. "And maybe we could include data from real-world case studies. I've read some reports about communities struggling with water contamination issues. If we show how our design addresses those challenges, it'll make our project even more compelling."

They spent the next hour brainstorming with Mr. Thornton, each idea building on the last. By the end of the meeting, they had a clear strategy: they would enhance their prototype to be as user-friendly and durable as possible, gather testimonials and real-world data, and create a presentation that focused on the lives their project could impact.

Over the following days, Dan and Brenda threw themselves into their work. They redesigned the prototype, focusing on three key aspects: durability, ease of use, and adaptability. After receiving feedback from Emma's nonprofit, they decided to replace some of the more delicate materials with sturdier alternatives that would withstand longer use in rough environments. They tested the filtration layers with different water samples, making careful adjustments to ensure consistency and effectiveness.

In addition to refining the prototype, they began reaching out to individuals and organizations they had connected with along the way. Emma agreed to provide a testimonial, speaking to the need for affordable water filtration systems in the communities her organization served. The teacher they had met at the regional contest also offered a statement, sharing her own experience with water scarcity and her admiration for their work.

To tie everything together, Brenda proposed creating a video that could serve as the introduction to their presentation. They wanted to show the human side of their project—the communities it was designed to help and the people who supported their mission.

They filmed scenes in their school lab, showing the testing process and the effort they put into refining each layer. They also included clips of local water sources, highlighting the need for clean water access even in their own area. As they edited the footage, Brenda added quotes from their supporters, weaving together a narrative that was both educational and heartfelt.

As the national contest date drew nearer, they began practicing their presentation with an intensity they hadn't experienced before. Mr. Thornton, along with a few other teachers, volunteered to watch their rehearsals, offering constructive feedback on everything from their posture to the pacing of their speech.

One afternoon, after a particularly intense practice session, Mr. Thornton called them aside.

"You two have come a long way since that first pitch," he said, his voice filled with pride. "Remember, nationals will be tough. The judges will ask difficult questions, and some of the other teams may have more resources at their disposal. But you have something special here. Don't lose sight of your mission."

Dan felt a swell of gratitude for their teacher's guidance. "Thank you, Mr. Thornton. We couldn't have done this without your support."

Brenda added, "We'll do our best. No matter what happens, we're proud of how far we've come."

The day of the national science contest arrived at last, and Dan and Brenda found themselves standing in front of a massive convention hall. The sheer scale of the event was overwhelming, with hundreds of students from all over the country setting up booths and preparing their presentations. The atmosphere buzzed with excitement and nerves, and the magnitude of the competition became palpable as they walked through the rows of projects.

They reached their assigned booth and began setting up their display. The centerpiece was, of course, their refined prototype, carefully arranged to show each layer and its function. They set up the tablet with their video introduction and arranged the testimonial posters around the table to create a cohesive presentation.

As they worked, they couldn't help but notice some of the neighboring booths. One team had built an artificial intelligence system for diagnosing medical conditions in remote areas. Another had developed a new method for converting waste into biofuel. The projects were cutting-edge, and the students running them looked confident and well-prepared.

Brenda leaned closer to Dan, whispering, "These projects are on another level. Do you think we stand a chance?"

Dan took a deep breath, feeling a mix of awe and determination. "Maybe they're more advanced in certain ways, but our project has something they don't. It's practical, it's accessible, and it can make a real difference. Let's focus on that."

They finished setting up just as the contest began, and soon after, the judges started making their rounds. Dan and Brenda watched as teams around them presented with polished precision, each project revealing a new level of creativity and technical expertise. As the judges approached their booth, they exchanged a final, reassuring glance.

The head judge, a woman with silver hair and a keen, focused gaze, introduced herself as Dr. Patel, a specialist in environmental science. Accompanying her were two other judges, both with backgrounds in engineering and public health.

Dr. Patel spoke first, her tone professional yet encouraging. "We're very interested in your water filtration project. Please, walk us through it."

Brenda began, explaining the inspiration behind their work and the importance of clean water access in underserved communities. She introduced the prototype, highlighting the simplicity of the design and the careful selection of materials to ensure affordability and effectiveness.

Dan followed, going into detail about each layer of the system and how they had optimized it for durability and ease of use. He shared the data they had collected, showing how their system reduced impurities in various types of water samples.

As they finished their presentation, Dr. Patel looked impressed. "This is a very well-thought-out design. What challenges did you face, and how did you overcome them?"

Dan didn't hesitate. "One of our biggest challenges was ensuring consistent quality across different material sources. We spent a lot of time testing to make sure each material met our standards, even when sourced from different locations."

Brenda added, "We also had to simplify the design so that it could be used in various environments. By creating a visual guide and adding color-coded layers, we made the system easier to assemble and maintain."

The judges continued to ask questions, probing into the technical aspects of the design, the feasibility of large-scale implementation, and the potential for improvements. Dan and Brenda answered each question with clarity, drawing from their extensive preparation and the lessons they had learned along the way.

Finally, Dr. Patel nodded approvingly. "Thank you both. You've done an excellent job of balancing scientific rigor with real-world impact. This project has a lot of potential."

After the judges moved on, Dan and Brenda shared a smile of relief. They had done it—they had presented their project to some of the top minds in their field, and it felt like their hard work had paid off.

THE SCIENCE CONTEST

The awards ceremony later that afternoon was filled with anticipation. The announcer began listing the winners for each category, and the crowd erupted into applause for each team that took the stage. Dan and Brenda held their breath, waiting as their category was announced.

"The award for Best Community and Environmental Impact goes to… Dan Carter and Brenda Collins!"

The applause was overwhelming as they made their way to the stage. They accepted the award, both feeling a profound sense of accomplishment and gratitude. Their journey had been long and challenging, but in that moment, it all felt worth it.

Chapter 11: The National Contest

The excitement of their victory at nationals gave Dan and Brenda an unparalleled confidence, but it also introduced them to a new level of pressure. Winning such a prestigious award validated their hard work and confirmed that their project had potential on a larger scale. Yet, they knew this recognition would only mean something if they could turn their filtration system into a real-world solution. The acclaim had opened doors, but it had also raised expectations—from themselves, their community, and now from potential sponsors.

Returning to school, Dan and Brenda were greeted by applause and cheers from their classmates and teachers. Mr. Thornton organized a small celebration in the science lab, where he presented them with a plaque commemorating their achievement. As they looked around at the faces of their supporters, they felt the weight of responsibility that came with their success.

During the celebration, Mr. Thornton pulled them aside, his expression both proud and thoughtful. "You've come so far," he said, his tone warm but serious. "But there's a long road ahead if you want to make this project a reality. Have you thought about what the next steps might be?"

Dan took a breath, glancing at Brenda. "We've thought about it. We know the design works, but it's still a prototype. If we want this to be used by actual communities, we'll need to find partners, refine the design even more, and probably look for funding."

Brenda added, "And we'll need to test it in real environments—places that actually need it. We want to prove that it's not just effective in a lab, but in the real world, where conditions aren't perfect."

Mr. Thornton gave them a nod of approval. "That's the right mindset. And I think I might know someone who can help you with this. A friend of mine works with a water research center in another state, and they have a community outreach program focused on clean water initiatives. I could arrange an introduction if you're interested."

Both Dan and Brenda immediately agreed, feeling a surge of excitement. The opportunity to connect with professionals in the field would be invaluable, especially if it could lead to real-world testing for their system.

A week later, they found themselves on a video call with Dr. Helen Carter, an experienced researcher who specialized in environmental engineering and community health. Dr. Carter's work had taken her to regions with severe water scarcity, and she had years of experience in developing water filtration solutions tailored to low-resource settings.

As they explained their project, Dr. Carter listened attentively, occasionally making notes. She was a woman in her fifties, with a warm smile and an analytical gaze that indicated she understood the challenges they were up against.

When they finished, she smiled approvingly. "I'm impressed. For high school students, you've shown remarkable insight and innovation. But if you want this system to be field-ready, you'll need to consider a few more factors."

Dan and Brenda listened closely as Dr. Carter outlined potential improvements. She suggested they consider how the filtration system would handle extreme weather, fluctuating water quality, and even natural contaminants like algae. She recommended experimenting with locally sourced materials to make the system truly scalable.

"Field testing is critical," Dr. Carter emphasized. "Until you've seen how it performs in an uncontrolled environment, you can't be sure it'll work reliably. The good news is, my center has several partner communities that would be open to testing your system. It'll take time and coordination, but I believe this could be a viable solution with the right support."

Her encouragement filled them with renewed determination. Over the next few weeks, they corresponded with Dr. Carter, sending her updates and working through her suggestions. She connected them with engineers and community leaders who offered feedback, and they adjusted their design based on the real-world insights they received.

They built several new prototypes, testing them with different types of water samples—ranging from muddy water collected from a local pond to runoff from a nearby field after heavy rain. Each test revealed new strengths and weaknesses, forcing them to make additional changes to strengthen the filtration and improve durability.

One afternoon, as they were testing their latest prototype, Dan shared a concern he'd been holding back. "Brenda, have you thought about what happens if this actually works? I mean, like if it gets picked up by an organization or a company. It could change everything."

Brenda considered his question, feeling both the excitement and the weight of it. "I have. And to be honest, that's exactly what I hope for. I don't want this to stay in a lab or as a project we made for a contest. If we can bring this to communities that need it, then it's all worth it."

Dan nodded, sharing her determination. "Then let's keep going. We've come this far; there's no turning back."

In the meantime, they faced a new challenge: funding. Their crowdfunding campaign had been successful enough to support their initial prototypes, but building more durable versions and conducting thorough field tests required additional resources. As they looked for funding options, they applied for several grants, hoping to find one that aligned with their mission.

After weeks of waiting, they received good news—one of their grant applications had been approved, awarding them enough funding to build several new prototypes and cover travel expenses for field tests. The grant came with one condition: they would need to document their progress meticulously and share updates with the grant committee, which would evaluate their results for potential further funding.

THE SCIENCE CONTEST

With new funding in hand, Dan and Brenda intensified their work, coordinating with Dr. Carter to arrange field tests in two communities identified as ideal for the initial trials. The first was a rural area with limited infrastructure, and the second was a small town with ongoing water contamination issues. Both communities had agreed to participate in the trial and provide feedback, a step that felt like the beginning of something real.

The day of their first field test arrived with a mix of nerves and excitement. Dan and Brenda traveled with Dr. Carter to the rural community, carrying their new prototypes and a supply of replacement materials. The journey was long, taking them down narrow, dusty roads lined with fields and small homes. When they arrived, they were greeted by a local leader named Mr. Alvarez, who had organized a small group of residents interested in the project.

Mr. Alvarez welcomed them warmly, shaking their hands with genuine appreciation. "Thank you for bringing this solution here. Clean water has always been a challenge, especially during the dry season. We're eager to see how your system works."

Dan and Brenda set up their prototypes near the main water source, a small well that served most of the community. The water from the well was murky, filled with sediment and organic matter. Brenda explained the filtration process to the residents, demonstrating each layer and how it worked. Dan showed them how to assemble the system, making sure they understood each step.

As they ran the first test, the residents watched intently, whispering to each other as the murky water began to clear. The system worked slowly, but after a few minutes, clear water trickled out, catching the sunlight as it pooled in a small cup. One of the women, an older resident named Rosa, took a sip, her eyes lighting up with relief.

"This tastes clean," Rosa said, her voice filled with wonder. "Thank you. This could make such a difference for us."

Hearing her words brought a powerful sense of accomplishment to Dan and Brenda. They knew this was just the beginning, but seeing the impact firsthand made all their struggles worthwhile.

In the following days, they monitored the filtration systems, training residents to maintain them and replace the layers as needed. They gathered feedback from the community, noting any issues that arose, from flow rate challenges to questions about filter longevity. The experience taught them more than they had anticipated, revealing both the strengths and areas for improvement in their design.

After completing the field test in the first community, they moved on to the small town, where the issues were more complex. The water here was chemically contaminated, requiring an additional filtration layer to neutralize certain pollutants. They worked with Dr. Carter to develop a simple attachment that could address the specific contaminants, testing it rigorously before introducing it to the residents.

By the time they completed their field tests, they had gathered extensive data and firsthand feedback from people who would be directly impacted by their project. Returning home, they felt a renewed sense of purpose. They had seen the potential of their work to change lives, and they were more motivated than ever to refine and expand their project.

Back at school, they presented their findings to Mr. Thornton, who listened with pride as they shared stories from the field and outlined the improvements they planned to make. He was particularly moved by the testimonials from residents, especially Rosa's words, which they had written down as a reminder of their mission.

Chapter 12: Going Beyond the Contest

Dan and Brenda's field testing in real communities marked a turning point. Their filtration system was no longer just a prototype confined to the school lab; it was a practical tool that could transform lives. After returning from the field, they faced a new challenge—how to turn their project into something sustainable and scalable. They realized that making a meaningful impact would require organizational support, partnerships, and a clear plan for growth.

The day after their return, they met in the school's science lab to discuss their next steps. Surrounded by their notes, data, and the updated prototype, they reviewed their findings, considering how each piece fit into the bigger picture.

"We've proven that the system works," Brenda said, scrolling through photos and feedback on her laptop. "But if we want to help more communities, we'll need more resources—funding, materials, and a team of people who understand the vision."

Dan leaned back, thinking. "We could try reaching out to organizations again. We've shown that it works in the field, so that might help us attract sponsors or partners."

Brenda looked over at him, her face lighting up with a new idea. "Or we could start an organization ourselves. Something small to begin with, just to manage the project and maybe handle a few partnerships. That way, we could maintain control and grow it gradually."

The idea resonated with both of them. Creating their own organization would allow them to develop the project on their terms, ensuring that the mission of making clean water accessible stayed at the forefront. They knew it would be a big commitment, but they were both ready for the challenge.

Later that day, they sat down with Mr. Thornton to share their idea. Their teacher listened with keen interest, nodding as they outlined their vision.

"I think it's an ambitious and brilliant idea," he said, his tone filled with encouragement. "Running an organization is challenging, but you both have the skills, passion, and now, the experience. I can help you get started, maybe even connect you with a few people who have expertise in nonprofit management."

Mr. Thornton went on to explain some of the basics of setting up a nonprofit organization, from drafting a mission statement to developing a strategic plan. Dan and Brenda took careful notes, realizing just how much they would need to learn.

They decided to call their organization **PureWater Initiative**, a name that captured both their purpose and their commitment to clean water access. Over the next few weeks, they worked on establishing the foundations of their organization. They wrote a mission statement, defined their goals, and outlined a preliminary plan for partnerships, funding, and outreach.

With Mr. Thornton's help, they drafted a proposal detailing their project's impact and potential for scalability. The proposal would serve as the basis for reaching out to potential supporters, from local businesses to larger organizations. They even created a website, with photos from their field tests, testimonials from the communities they'd worked with, and a description of their mission.

Brenda took charge of crafting the website's narrative, capturing the heart of their story. She wrote about their journey, the challenges they'd faced, and the moments that had inspired them to continue. Dan handled the technical details, setting up donation links and organizing the data they would share with visitors.

Once their website and proposal were ready, they began reaching out to contacts they had made through their contests and fieldwork. Emma from the nonprofit was one of their first supporters, and she agreed to help spread the word among her networks. With her endorsement and the connections they'd formed along the way, they slowly started to attract attention.

One evening, as they were reviewing responses to their proposal, Brenda received an email from a community foundation that specialized in environmental projects. The foundation was interested in funding a pilot program for the PureWater Initiative, offering them the resources to bring their filtration systems to five more communities over the next year.

Brenda's excitement was contagious as she read the email aloud to Dan. "This could be huge! With their support, we could scale up our project and reach more people."

Dan felt a surge of excitement and a hint of nervousness. "We'd need to manage all aspects of the rollout—distribution, training, and maintenance. This isn't just another test; it's a full-scale pilot."

They knew that the opportunity was too valuable to pass up. After discussing the details, they agreed to a meeting with the foundation's representatives to outline their plan and expectations. In preparation, they spent days refining their prototype even further, working on the logistics of transporting the filtration systems and developing a detailed training guide for each community.

The meeting with the foundation took place in a conference room at a nearby office. Dan and Brenda arrived early, setting up their materials and rehearsing their presentation one last time. The representatives from the foundation—a group of three experienced professionals—listened attentively as Dan and Brenda presented their pilot program, explaining how the filtration systems would be introduced, supported, and monitored in each community.

After a series of in-depth questions, the foundation representatives expressed their support. "We're impressed by your commitment and the thoroughness of your planning," said the director, a woman named Ms. Reyes. "We're confident that with our funding and your expertise, this project has the potential to make a real difference."

When they left the meeting with a signed agreement, Dan and Brenda could hardly contain their excitement. They had secured the support they needed to bring their project to a new level, and the months of hard work were finally paying off.

The following weeks were a whirlwind of activity as they prepared to launch their pilot program. They ordered materials in bulk, working with suppliers to ensure consistent quality and cost-effectiveness. They also connected with leaders in each of the five chosen communities, coordinating logistics and setting up training sessions.

For each community, they prepared a tailored plan, ensuring that every participant understood the system and could maintain it independently. Brenda crafted simplified guides with clear visuals, and Dan worked on developing a support system through phone calls and video tutorials to address any issues as they arose.

As the pilot program launched, they visited each community, working closely with residents to install the filtration systems and train them on their use and upkeep. The experience was both rewarding and challenging, as each community presented unique needs and conditions. Some systems needed additional adjustments to function optimally, while others required minor tweaks to improve durability in harsher environments.

In one community, they encountered an unexpected challenge with sediment buildup that clogged the filter faster than anticipated. Dan and Brenda worked alongside the residents, experimenting with different solutions until they found an effective adjustment. The experience taught them the importance of adaptability, reminding them that every solution needed to be flexible to meet varying conditions.

Throughout the pilot program, they documented their progress, gathering feedback and refining their approach. Each successful test, each improvement, and each smile from a resident reminded them of why they had started this journey in the first place.

Months passed, and the PureWater Initiative began to attract even more attention. With the foundation's support, they reached out to other nonprofits, environmental groups, and businesses interested in supporting clean water access. Their pilot program became a model, inspiring others to explore simple, affordable solutions for water filtration.

In addition to scaling up their operations, they began attending environmental conferences, where they presented their project and shared their story. Their presence in the field and the success of the pilot program resonated with audiences, drawing interest from journalists and advocates alike.

Chapter 13: Growing Pains

The PureWater Initiative was making strides, but as Dan and Brenda dove deeper into the world of nonprofits and field operations, they encountered a host of new challenges. Scaling a project to serve multiple communities required a level of management and organization they hadn't anticipated. What had started as a passion project was now developing into a full-fledged organization, and with that growth came unforeseen complexities.

In the beginning, PureWater had only required Dan and Brenda's combined efforts. But now, as interest and demand for their water filtration system grew, they found themselves overwhelmed. From managing logistics to coordinating with local community leaders, they were constantly balancing different tasks, and their schoolwork was beginning to suffer as a result.

One morning, as they reviewed their growing list of responsibilities in the school library, Brenda sighed, tapping her pen on the table thoughtfully.

"Dan, we're spread too thin. We've got requests coming in from other communities, plus the foundation's updates, and our grant applications. Not to mention our actual schoolwork. I'm starting to feel like we're barely keeping up."

Dan ran a hand through his hair, visibly frustrated. "I know. And every time we make progress, it feels like there's ten new things added to our to-do list. I don't want to let anyone down, but we need help."

They both knew they couldn't handle everything on their own. It was time to bring in more people, to expand their team and share the workload. Yet finding the right people—people who were as dedicated to the cause as they were—would be a challenge in itself.

The next day, they sat down with Mr. Thornton to discuss their options. He listened to their concerns, nodding thoughtfully as they described the pressures they were facing.

"You're both in a stage of growth that can be difficult for any organization, especially one led by students," he said. "But you're at a point where building a team is not just necessary—it's essential if you want to keep this project sustainable."

Brenda looked at Dan, her expression uncertain. "We were thinking of asking a few classmates to help, but we're not sure who would be as invested in this as we are."

Mr. Thornton smiled. "You might be surprised. People are drawn to projects with purpose, and PureWater has that in spades. Start with those you know, people you trust and who have skills that complement yours. Then, once you have a team, assign clear roles and responsibilities. It'll help everyone stay focused."

They left the meeting feeling optimistic, with a plan to recruit a small team of dedicated volunteers who could handle different aspects of PureWater. Brenda began drafting an announcement for their school's environmental club, hoping to attract students interested in sustainable solutions. Meanwhile, Dan created a list of skills they needed, including social media management, logistics, and data analysis.

Within a week, they held their first PureWater team meeting. Five students from the environmental club had signed up to help, and Dan and Brenda briefed them on the organization's mission, goals, and the challenges they were facing. Each new team member brought something unique to the table: Mira, who had a knack for organization and logistics; Leo, a tech enthusiast who offered to handle social media; Amy, who was passionate about community outreach; and two others, Josh and Lia, who were interested in assisting with data collection and fieldwork.

During that initial meeting, Dan and Brenda outlined the team's responsibilities and discussed their upcoming projects. They felt a renewed sense of purpose seeing the enthusiasm in their new teammates' faces, realizing that PureWater's mission was resonating with others.

"We're grateful for everyone's help," Brenda said as they wrapped up. "This project has grown faster than we ever expected, but with all of you here, I think we can handle it."

Mira grinned. "We're ready to help in any way we can. This is an amazing cause, and we're honored to be part of it."

With their new team in place, Dan and Brenda divided responsibilities and focused on training everyone. The team members quickly took to their roles, and having extra hands made a noticeable difference. Mira proved to be a natural at logistics, efficiently coordinating shipments of materials and organizing field trips. Leo's social media efforts brought new attention to PureWater's work, increasing their following and attracting small donations from supporters across the country.

Despite the progress, however, managing a growing team brought new challenges. Decisions that had once been simple for Dan and Brenda now required group discussions, and disagreements occasionally arose over priorities and strategies. One afternoon, as they prepared for a field test, a heated debate broke out between Leo and Amy over the organization's messaging on social media.

"I just think we should focus more on the environmental impact," Leo argued. "We're trying to promote sustainable solutions, and the environmental aspect is huge."

Amy disagreed, her tone passionate. "But the social impact is equally important! This project is about helping people in need, and that should be the main focus."

Dan tried to mediate, feeling the tension rise in the room. "I think you're both right. Maybe we can find a balance that highlights both aspects?"

Brenda chimed in, reinforcing Dan's point. "Exactly. This project is about environmental sustainability, but it's also about supporting communities. Let's find a way to showcase both without losing the essence of our mission."

The meeting continued, and though they reached a compromise, it was clear that managing a team required more patience and diplomacy than Dan and Brenda had anticipated. They were learning that leadership meant finding common ground and guiding the team through differences, all while staying focused on the bigger picture.

As the months went on, PureWater gained momentum. They secured additional funding, expanded their pilot program to new communities, and began developing partnerships with environmental organizations and local governments. But as the project grew, so did the strain on Dan and Brenda's partnership. They found themselves disagreeing more often, their perspectives on the organization's future diverging in subtle but significant ways.

One evening, after a particularly challenging meeting with the team, Brenda confronted Dan, her voice filled with frustration.

"Dan, I feel like we're not on the same page anymore. You keep pushing for us to expand faster, but I think we need to focus on quality over quantity. We can't help more communities if the systems we're providing aren't perfect."

Dan frowned, struggling to keep his own frustration in check. "I get it, Brenda, but we have a responsibility to meet the demand. Every day we delay means more people going without clean water. We can't just stop now."

Their disagreement lingered, each of them convinced of their perspective. They both cared deeply about the mission, but their different approaches were creating tension, and neither was willing to compromise easily.

As the days passed, the strain began affecting their work. Brenda started focusing more on refining the design, making sure every detail was flawless, while Dan concentrated on expanding PureWater's reach. They found themselves working separately more often, with less communication than before, and the organization's goals seemed to blur as their visions diverged.

Mr. Thornton noticed the growing rift between them and invited them to his classroom one afternoon. He listened as they each voiced their concerns, allowing them to express their frustrations openly.

"Dan, Brenda," he began after they had finished, "it's clear that you both care deeply about PureWater, but every organization faces growing pains. This disagreement is a sign that PureWater is evolving, and so are both of you. Leadership isn't just about moving forward—it's about staying connected to your mission and each other."

Brenda looked at Dan, her expression softening. "Maybe we've both been so focused on our own ideas that we forgot why we started this project in the first place."

Dan nodded, his frustration dissipating. "You're right. I've been pushing for expansion, but I don't want to lose sight of the quality and purpose we built PureWater on. Let's find a way to balance both."

With Mr. Thornton's guidance, they spent the next hour discussing their goals and finding common ground. They agreed that while growth was important, maintaining quality was equally essential. They decided to prioritize perfecting the filtration system before expanding further and committed to keeping each other updated on all major decisions.

The renewed understanding between them breathed new life into their partnership. They began collaborating closely again, blending Brenda's focus on quality with Dan's drive for expansion. Their team noticed the difference, and the sense of purpose within PureWater strengthened, each member now fully aligned with their mission.

With their foundation more solid than ever, Dan and Brenda moved forward with a clear plan. They refined their filtration system to be more durable and efficient, incorporating feedback from field tests and community members. They improved their training guides, ensuring they were easy to understand, and made adjustments to accommodate different types of water sources.

The months of hard work paid off, and PureWater's reputation grew. They were invited to present at conferences, featured in local news, and even received inquiries from international organizations interested in adapting the model for other regions. Their team continued to expand, attracting passionate volunteers and advisors who believed in the mission.

Chapter 14: Launch Day

Months of hard work, persistence, and problem-solving had brought Dan and Brenda to an incredible milestone—the official launch of the PureWater Initiative. Today wasn't just about celebrating the impact they'd already achieved; it was about marking the beginning of their mission's reach beyond what they'd ever imagined.

The launch was held in the community center of the town where they'd conducted their first successful pilot. Community leaders, nonprofit representatives, teachers, and supporters filled the room, all eager to learn about PureWater's journey and the lives it aimed to improve. Even some local media outlets were present to capture the event, bringing attention to the young innovators who had turned a high school project into something transformative.

As they stood at the entrance, greeting guests and answering questions, Dan and Brenda felt a mix of excitement and nervous energy. They had planned every detail, from the presentation to a demonstration of the latest prototype, but the reality of sharing their work on such a public platform made the moment feel monumental.

"Ready?" Dan asked, glancing over at Brenda. His voice carried a hint of nerves, but his expression was one of determination.

Brenda smiled, feeling a wave of gratitude for their journey together. "Ready as I'll ever be. Let's show them what PureWater is all about."

The event began with Mr. Thornton introducing them to the crowd. His words were filled with pride and admiration, recounting how he'd seen Dan and Brenda's project evolve from a simple science contest entry to an initiative that had touched the lives of real people.

"These two students represent the very best of what it means to use knowledge for a greater good," he said, his voice resonating through the room. "Their dedication to this cause has brought clean water to communities in need and has shown us all what's possible when young people put their minds to making a difference."

After his introduction, Dan and Brenda took the stage, the weight of the moment sinking in as they faced the expectant crowd. They shared the story of how PureWater had begun as a solution to a basic problem, born from a simple desire to make clean water accessible to everyone. They recounted the obstacles they'd faced along the way—the challenges of scaling, the disagreements, the field tests, and the learning curve of running an organization. But more than anything, they emphasized the people who had supported them and believed in their mission.

"We couldn't have come this far alone," Dan said, looking out at the crowd. "Every step of the journey has been shaped by the people who believed in us, who encouraged us to keep going even when things got tough. PureWater isn't just our project; it's a shared vision that belongs to all of you."

Brenda took a deep breath, her voice steady but filled with emotion. "And today, we're here to launch this initiative, knowing that it's only the beginning. We want to continue growing, reaching more communities, and providing a tool that empowers people to access something as essential as clean water."

The crowd erupted in applause, the energy of their support filling the room. Dan and Brenda shared a quiet moment of pride and relief, knowing they had conveyed the heart of their mission to the audience.

Following their presentation, they invited guests to visit a demonstration area where they had set up their latest filtration prototype. It was larger and more durable than the initial models, designed to handle higher volumes of water for larger communities. Each layer of the system was carefully labeled, and a clear glass container at the bottom displayed the purified water that came out of the system.

Community members, especially those from areas that had used the earlier prototypes, examined the filtration system with curiosity. Some asked questions about how it worked, while others shared their own experiences with the filtration systems in their villages.

One of the community leaders, Mr. Alvarez, stepped forward, a smile on his face. "I remember when you first brought this to our village," he said, addressing Dan and Brenda. "It's made a huge difference in our lives. Families who once struggled to find clean water now have a reliable solution. On behalf of everyone, thank you for what you've done."

Hearing his words, Brenda felt a swell of emotion, grateful for the impact they had made. Each story of how the filtration systems had improved daily life reinforced their commitment to continuing the work.

As the day continued, they noticed a man in a suit observing the prototype intently, occasionally scribbling in a notebook. Intrigued, Dan approached him, introducing himself and sharing a bit about the project.

The man introduced himself as Mr. Greene, a representative from a major environmental organization that supported sustainable water projects worldwide. He had heard about PureWater and wanted to learn more.

"I'm impressed by what you've done here," Mr. Greene said, his tone thoughtful. "Your design is practical and scalable, two things that many projects often miss. And most importantly, you've made it accessible to communities that don't have extensive resources."

Dan's excitement grew as Mr. Greene continued, explaining that his organization was interested in supporting projects like PureWater and that they might be able to provide both funding and technical resources for future expansions.

Brenda joined them, listening with interest as Mr. Greene outlined potential areas where they could collaborate. The prospect of partnering with a larger organization was thrilling, especially one with experience and connections in the environmental sector. They exchanged contact information, promising to follow up on the possibilities.

After Mr. Greene walked away, Brenda turned to Dan, a smile spreading across her face. "Can you believe that? If this works out, PureWater could reach even more communities, maybe even internationally."

Dan felt a surge of pride. "I think we're finally getting to a place where we can make a real impact. This could change everything."

As the event wrapped up, Dan and Brenda took a moment to reflect. Standing in the now-empty room, surrounded by the remnants of their display and a handful of leftover materials, they were struck by the enormity of what they had achieved.

"It feels surreal," Brenda said quietly, her gaze distant. "We started this just hoping to make a difference, and now look at what it's become. We've actually created something that matters."

Dan nodded, feeling the same sense of wonder. "Yeah. And the best part is, this is just the beginning. We're only getting started."

They began packing up, chatting about the feedback they had received and the connections they had made. Mr. Thornton came over, his expression filled with pride as he congratulated them once more.

"You two have accomplished something remarkable," he said. "And I have no doubt that PureWater will continue to grow, thanks to your dedication."

Brenda smiled, feeling the warmth of his support. "Thank you, Mr. Thornton. We couldn't have done this without you."

Dan added, "You've been with us since the beginning, guiding us every step of the way. We owe so much of this to you."

Mr. Thornton waved a hand dismissively, though his smile betrayed his pride. "You both had the vision and the drive. I was just here to support you."

As they finished packing, Mr. Greene approached them once more, his expression thoughtful. "I wanted to mention something before I go," he said. "Our organization runs an annual summit on clean water access, and we invite innovators from around the world to present their solutions. I think PureWater would be a fantastic addition to this year's summit, if you're interested."

Brenda's eyes widened. "That sounds incredible! We'd love to be a part of it."

Dan agreed enthusiastically, recognizing the summit as a chance to showcase PureWater on an international platform. They arranged to discuss the details in the coming weeks, their excitement renewed by this unexpected opportunity.

Chapter 15: The Global Summit

The invitation to present PureWater at the international clean water summit felt like a dream come true. Dan and Brenda had worked tirelessly, and the chance to showcase their project on a global platform was an opportunity they'd never imagined. They knew this was more than just another presentation; it was a chance to inspire others, attract support, and ultimately expand PureWater to reach even more communities.

The summit was held in Geneva, Switzerland, in a grand conference center overlooking the city. For Dan and Brenda, just being there was a surreal experience. They were surrounded by renowned scientists, engineers, environmental activists, and policymakers from all over the world, each bringing their own innovative solutions for water accessibility and sustainability.

Mr. Greene's organization had sponsored their travel and lodging, giving them access to a level of exposure and resources they had only dreamed of. As they entered the hall on the first day, they were struck by the diversity and scope of the projects around them—water desalination technologies, renewable energy-powered pumps, and even genetically engineered algae to filter water.

In the midst of such sophisticated technology, their simple but effective filtration system felt small. Yet they reminded themselves that PureWater's strength lay in its accessibility. Unlike some of the other high-tech solutions, theirs was affordable and could be implemented with minimal resources—a solution that could work in any rural village or underserved community without complicated infrastructure.

On the day of their presentation, Dan and Brenda set up their booth with meticulous care. They brought their latest prototype, larger and sturdier than the previous models, and displayed posters that illustrated the filtration process and highlighted the feedback they had received from communities. They also set up a video showing testimonials from community members who had used the system, a powerful reminder of the impact they had already achieved.

As the summit attendees began circulating, many stopped by to learn more about PureWater. Some were curious about the mechanics of the filtration layers, while others wanted to know how it compared to more complex systems. Dan and Brenda took turns explaining their design, each interaction deepening their confidence and their commitment to their mission.

One visitor, a researcher from Kenya named Dr. Mbeki, listened closely as Dan described the materials they used and the testing they'd done in various communities.

"This is brilliant in its simplicity," Dr. Mbeki said, clearly impressed. "In many of our villages, access to clean water is an ongoing struggle, but many of the solutions available are either too expensive or too difficult to maintain. Your system seems like it could be adapted to work in a variety of settings."

Brenda felt a surge of excitement. "That's exactly what we're hoping for—to create something people can use without needing advanced technology or special skills."

Dr. Mbeki offered his contact information, suggesting a potential collaboration between PureWater and his organization back in Africa. "If you're ever able to expand internationally, I'd be thrilled to help introduce this system to our communities. I believe it could make a real difference."

They exchanged information, and as he walked away, Brenda turned to Dan, a smile spreading across her face. "This is it, Dan. We're finally connecting with people who want to bring PureWater beyond our borders."

Dan nodded, feeling the magnitude of the moment. "It feels like everything we've worked for is starting to fall into place. But I know we still have a lot to learn."

THE SCIENCE CONTEST

Their main presentation was scheduled for the following day. It was to take place in a large auditorium filled with professionals from diverse fields, each dedicated to clean water solutions. The stakes felt higher than ever, and the night before, they rehearsed every detail, running through their slides, refining their words, and anticipating questions from the audience.

That night, neither of them slept much. The pressure weighed heavily, but they reminded themselves of their purpose: this was about making clean water accessible, about showing the world that an affordable solution could transform lives.

When their presentation time finally arrived, they took the stage, standing side by side under the bright lights. The audience was silent, their attention focused entirely on the two young innovators who had turned a high school science project into a tool for social change.

Brenda began with the story of how they'd developed the idea, sharing the inspiration behind their design and the challenges they had faced along the way. She spoke about the communities they had visited, the lives they had touched, and the sense of purpose that had driven them to keep going, even when things seemed impossible.

Dan followed, detailing the mechanics of the filtration system, explaining each layer's function and how they had refined the design based on field testing and community feedback. He emphasized the accessibility and adaptability of the system, stressing that it was a solution that could work in a variety of settings.

To conclude, they played the video featuring testimonials from the communities that had benefited from PureWater. The screen showed smiles, laughter, and genuine gratitude from the residents who had seen firsthand the difference clean water could make in their daily lives. The room was silent, many in the audience visibly moved by the stories.

As the video ended, Brenda turned to the audience, her voice filled with conviction. "PureWater started as a simple idea, but it has become something much more—a tool for change, a way to bridge the gap between need and access. We believe that everyone deserves clean water, and we hope that with your support, we can continue to bring PureWater to more communities around the world."

Applause erupted, filling the auditorium. Dan and Brenda exchanged a relieved glance, feeling a wave of pride and gratitude. They had shared their vision, and it had resonated.

After their presentation, they were approached by representatives from several organizations interested in learning more. Some offered advice, while others discussed potential partnerships, eager to explore ways to support and expand PureWater's reach.

One representative from a large environmental foundation expressed interest in funding a pilot program to bring PureWater to several rural communities in South America. The possibility of such a collaboration was thrilling, and Dan and Brenda could hardly believe that their small project was gaining traction on a global scale.

As the summit continued, they found themselves connecting with people from all walks of life—scientists, activists, philanthropists, and even government officials. Each interaction opened new doors, and by the end of the summit, they had a list of contacts and partnership opportunities that would allow them to bring PureWater to more regions than they had ever dreamed possible.

On their last evening in Geneva, Dan and Brenda sat on a bench overlooking Lake Geneva, watching the sunset reflect off the water. The magnitude of the past few days was starting to sink in, and they felt both exhilarated and a little overwhelmed.

"It feels surreal," Dan said, his voice filled with wonder. "A few years ago, we were just two students with an idea. Now we're here, and it feels like PureWater is ready to reach the world."

Brenda nodded, a soft smile on her face. "It's incredible to think about how far we've come. But I know there's so much more to do."

They sat in comfortable silence for a while, each reflecting on the journey that had brought them to this point. PureWater had become a part of their lives in ways they hadn't anticipated. It had taught them resilience, teamwork, and the power of a shared vision. More than anything, it had given them a purpose that went beyond themselves.

Dan broke the silence, his tone thoughtful. "Do you think we'll keep doing this, even after college? I mean, could this be our lives—continuing PureWater and making it something lasting?"

Brenda looked at him, her expression filled with certainty. "I can't imagine doing anything else. PureWater is a part of us now. We've built something that matters, something that can keep making a difference. And as long as there are people who need clean water, I think we'll keep going."

They made a silent promise that night—a commitment to their mission and to each other. They knew that there would be more challenges, more moments of doubt, and perhaps even failures along the way. But they also knew that they had the strength and the vision to overcome them.

As they boarded the plane back home, they carried with them more than just memories of the summit. They brought back hope, plans, and a renewed sense of purpose. They were no longer just students; they were founders of an initiative that had the potential to change lives across the world.

Their journey had only just begun, and as they looked forward, they saw a future where PureWater continued to grow, reach, and transform. They were ready for whatever came next, ready to face each new challenge, and ready to keep moving forward, one community at a time.

Together, they would continue to build a legacy of impact, proving that with vision, dedication, and a little bit of hope, even the simplest ideas could change the world.

Chapter 16: A Lasting Legacy

Returning home from Geneva marked a new chapter not just for PureWater but for Dan and Brenda as well. They had achieved international recognition, secured partnerships, and laid the groundwork for an organization that could impact communities worldwide. But now, as they stood on the brink of adulthood with college on the horizon, they faced the challenge of balancing their personal futures with the mission they had built together.

As they prepared for college applications, scholarship essays, and final exams, Dan and Brenda spent long evenings discussing the future of PureWater. They were both dedicated to its success, but they knew they would soon be in different places, facing new responsibilities and commitments. For the first time, the question of how they would continue PureWater with limited time and resources loomed large.

One evening, after a particularly intense study session in the library, Dan looked up from his notes, his expression thoughtful.

"Brenda, we've come so far, and I can't imagine not being part of PureWater. But with college coming up, how are we going to make it work? I don't want this to become something we put aside or abandon."

Brenda leaned back, contemplating his words. "I've been thinking about that too. We need a plan—something sustainable. Maybe we can delegate some of the responsibilities, build a team that can handle the day-to-day operations while we focus on our studies. It would mean stepping back a bit, but it might be the only way to keep things moving forward."

They realized that their best option was to expand the PureWater team, bringing in people who could help manage and grow the organization while they pursued their studies. Over the next few weeks, they worked on recruiting a mix of passionate volunteers and experienced advisors, focusing on individuals who believed in PureWater's mission and had the skills to carry it forward.

THE SCIENCE CONTEST

Through their connections from the summit and the support of Mr. Thornton, they were able to find professionals with backgrounds in environmental science, nonprofit management, and fundraising who were eager to contribute. These new team members brought fresh perspectives and experience, helping to shape PureWater's structure and plan for expansion.

One of their first hires was a project coordinator named Sofia, a recent college graduate who had studied environmental management and shared a deep commitment to sustainable solutions. Sofia quickly became an invaluable part of the team, organizing logistics, coordinating with community partners, and keeping everyone on track.

With Sofia's help, Dan and Brenda were able to establish a sustainable framework for PureWater, setting clear goals and defining roles within the organization. They worked with her to streamline communication with community partners, create an online training module for local leaders, and establish regular updates for donors and supporters.

Sofia's presence allowed Dan and Brenda to begin stepping back from the daily operations, confident that PureWater was in capable hands. Though it was difficult to let go of some responsibilities, they knew it was necessary for the organization to grow independently. This transition also freed up their time to focus on their studies and prepare for the next phase of their lives.

As they neared graduation, they planned one final event to celebrate their journey with the people who had supported them from the beginning. They organized a community gathering at the school, inviting friends, family, teachers, local partners, and some of the community leaders they had worked with. The evening was a tribute not only to PureWater's success but also to the collective effort that had made it possible.

The event began with a presentation showcasing PureWater's progress, including the impact they had made in different communities and their goals for the future. Sofia spoke about the organization's recent achievements, emphasizing the importance of local partnerships and community involvement.

Dan and Brenda each took a moment to speak, reflecting on the journey that had started as a simple high school project and grown into a full-fledged organization. They shared stories from their field tests, the challenges they had faced, and the sense of purpose that had driven them to keep going.

"We started PureWater because we believed everyone deserved access to clean water," Dan said, his voice filled with pride. "But we could never have achieved this alone. This organization is as much yours as it is ours, and we're excited to see where it goes from here."

Brenda followed, her tone sincere and grateful. "This journey has taught us more than we ever could have imagined—about resilience, teamwork, and the power of community. We're so grateful for everyone who's been part of it, and we know that PureWater will continue to grow, long after we graduate."

Mr. Thornton then took the stage, his voice filled with pride as he spoke about Dan and Brenda's dedication and the legacy they were leaving behind.

"These two have shown us what's possible when passion and purpose come together," he said, glancing at Dan and Brenda. "They've inspired all of us, and I have no doubt that their impact will only continue to grow."

As the evening continued, guests mingled, sharing memories and congratulating Dan and Brenda on their success. They received heartfelt messages from community members whose lives had been touched by PureWater, as well as words of encouragement from friends and family who had witnessed their journey from the beginning.

At the end of the event, Dan and Brenda stood by the door, thanking each guest for their support. As the last few people left, they took a moment to reflect on the significance of the evening. It was a bittersweet moment, filled with pride and a sense of closure.

"Can you believe it?" Dan said, looking around the now-empty hall. "It feels like we're closing a chapter."

Brenda nodded, a soft smile on her face. "But it's a chapter that we'll carry with us. And PureWater will keep growing, even if we're not here every day to see it."

They knew that the future held unknowns, but they were confident in the foundation they had built. PureWater was more than just an organization; it was a legacy they had created together, one that would continue to impact lives long after they had moved on.

After the event, as they approached graduation, Dan and Brenda began preparing for college. They both had received offers from universities with strong environmental science and engineering programs, a testament to the work they had done with PureWater. Their experiences had shaped not only their careers but also their aspirations for the future.

Before they left for college, they met with Sofia one last time, reviewing PureWater's plans and discussing her role in leading the organization. She reassured them of her commitment, promising to stay true to their mission and keep them updated on PureWater's progress.

"I'll make sure PureWater continues to grow," Sofia said, her tone steady and determined. "This project means a lot to me, and I want to see it succeed as much as you do."

Dan and Brenda felt a sense of relief, knowing that PureWater was in good hands. They had built something strong, something that could stand on its own, and they were ready to pass the torch.

As they embarked on their college journeys, Dan and Brenda stayed in touch, regularly checking in with Sofia and following

PureWater's progress from afar. They watched as the organization expanded to new regions, partnered with additional nonprofits, and refined its model based on feedback from the field. Every update, every new community reached, was a reminder of the impact they had started.

PureWater's growth continued over the years, and as Dan and Brenda pursued their own paths, they remained connected to the organization, occasionally attending events or offering guidance when needed. The knowledge that PureWater was thriving without them was both humbling and deeply fulfilling.

One day, a few years after graduation, they received an invitation to attend a PureWater anniversary celebration, commemorating a decade of impact. The event brought together dozens of people from different backgrounds—community leaders, volunteers, partners, and even new generations of high school students who had joined PureWater's mission.

As Dan and Brenda walked into the event, they were struck by the scale of what PureWater had become. The small, grassroots project they had started had grown into a thriving organization with a global reach, touching lives across continents.

They met Sofia, now the executive director, who greeted them with a warm smile and a heartfelt hug. She led them around, introducing them to the team members, supporters, and community partners who had all contributed to PureWater's success.

During the event, Sofia invited Dan and Brenda to say a few words. Standing on the stage, looking out at the faces of those who had carried PureWater forward, they felt a deep sense of pride and gratitude.

"We're honored to be here today," Dan said, his voice filled with emotion. "PureWater began as a small idea, but it became something bigger than we could have ever imagined. It's not just about us anymore; it's about everyone here, everyone who has made this possible."

Brenda followed, her voice steady and sincere. "PureWater's mission was always about bringing clean water to those who need it most. Seeing what it's become, knowing that it's reached so many people—it's a dream come true. Thank you for keeping this vision alive and making it your own."

The applause was thunderous, and as Dan and Brenda stepped down from the stage, they felt a sense of closure. They had created something lasting, something that would continue to inspire and uplift.

They looked around the room filled with people who believed in PureWater's mission knowing that their journey had come full circle. They had set out to make a difference, and in doing so, they had left a legacy—proof that even the simplest ideas, when fueled by passion and purpose, could change the world.